He covered her hand, giving her fingers a little squeeze. "I like you, too," he said.

He liked her. A perfectly innocuous and friendly statement, certainly nothing that should make her pulse leap this way. Hadn't she just told him that she liked him, too? It was ridiculous for her to feel this schoolgirl breathlessness over such an innocent comment.

And yet there was nothing innocent about the gleam in his eyes when they lowered slowly from her own, pausing to study her mouth as if memorizing the contours. She could almost taste him again now— which only fueled her hunger for another sample.

Dear Reader,

I've had such a great time writing the DOCTORS IN TRAINING series, getting to know the five members of the study group I introduced in the first book, *Diagnosis Daddy*. I have to admit my favorite part of creating this series was all the time I spent quizzing my medical-resident daughter about her experiences in med school. She was so helpful, and we had a lot of fun dreaming up "what ifs." Any errors or embellishments, of course, have been all mine—but I'm very grateful for her assistance.

As graduation approaches, only one member of the study group is single and unattached. As happy as he is for his friends, James Stillman isn't sure there's a woman out there who's just right for him...until he meets free-spirited Shannon Gambill. Now his only problem is convincing Shannon that giving up her heart does not mean giving up her independence! I hope you enjoy their story.

Gina Wilkins

PROGNOSIS: ROMANCE

GINA WILKINS

SPECIAL EDITION®

Published by Silhouette Books

America's Publisher of Contemporary Romance

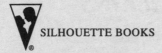 SILHOUETTE BOOKS

Recycling programs
for this product may
not exist in your area.

ISBN-13: 978-0-373-65551-9

PROGNOSIS: ROMANCE

Visit Silhouette Books at www.eHarlequin.com

Printed in U.S.A.

Books by Gina Wilkins

GINA WILKINS

is a bestselling and award-winning author who has written more than seventy novels for Harlequin and Silhouette Books. She credits her successful career in romance to her long, happy marriage and her three "extraordinary" children.

A lifelong resident of central Arkansas, Ms. Wilkins sold her first book to Harlequin in 1987 and has been writing full-time since. She has appeared on the Waldenbooks, B. Dalton and *USA TODAY* bestseller lists. She is a three-time recipient of the Maggie Award for Excellence, sponsored by Georgia Romance Writers, and has won several awards from the reviewers of *RT Book Reviews*.

For my agent, Denise Marcil,
in celebration of our silver anniversary of
working together. What a great journey it has been!

Chapter One

"Aunt Shannon, watch me!"

"Aunt Shannon, catch!"

"Aunt Shannon, I'm swimming. See?"

"Aunt Shannon, Aunt Shannon!"

The woman who was obviously "Aunt Shannon" laughed as she turned from one side to another in the hip-deep water of the lake, trying to respond to the half dozen children competing for her attention. From his lounge chair in a shady spot on the beach nearby, James Stillman watched her in fascination.

Somewhere in her mid- to late-twenties, she wasn't exactly beautiful, though he found the expressive face framed by a mop of red curls to be very intriguing. She looked a little familiar, but he couldn't remember ever meeting her before—and he couldn't imagine that he would have forgotten if he had.

Her slender body was nicely displayed in a bright yellow

bikini that bared just the right amount of fair skin to be neither too modest nor too brazen. He hoped she was wearing sunscreen. Though it was late afternoon and the most dangerous UV rays were beginning to fade, it was still sunny enough to cause a burn if she wasn't careful.

Or was that just the scientist in him fretting? He'd been accused many times of being too serious about everything.

He watched as the woman picked up a little boy and tossed him a few feet away into the water. The boy, who might have been three or four, bobbed to the surface sputtering with giggles. He begged, "Do it again, Aunt Shannon!"

"No, me. Me," a little girl of perhaps five insisted. Splashing from within the confines of a snug yellow-and-orange life vest, she dog-paddled ahead of him. "Throw me, Aunt Shannon."

A brunette woman, lounging on a towel not far from where James sat, looked in that direction momentarily taking her attention from the thick paperback in her hands. A ginger-haired man dozed beside her. "Jack. Caitlin. Settle down," she called out, then returned her gaze to her book.

Her words had no visible effect on the children, who continued begging their aunt to play with them. Another boy, maybe seven or eight, floated on a neon-blue air mattress a few feet deeper in the water. He splashed his arms vigorously to propel the mattress forward, calling for Shannon to admire his navigational skills.

A girl who appeared to be about the same age as the boy on the raft tossed a purple beach ball into the waves, then swam to retrieve it. Occasionally she threw it at Shannon, who caught it deftly and lobbed it back. Two other girls, obviously twins, whom James estimated to be about ten years old, played nearby, vying to see who could float the longest without dropping her legs. They called out regularly for Shannon to determine the winner.

All of the children surrounding her had some shade of red hair, he noted. There were a few other families playing in the designated swimming area of the popular central Arkansas lake, but they were farther down the beach, giving Shannon and her boisterous nieces and nephews plenty of room to frolic. Brightly colored buoys strung together with yellow cording marked off the generous swimming area, protecting it from the ski boats and fishing boats skimming past on the lake and leaving behind waves to delight the swimmers.

From somewhere behind James, another red-haired woman who resembled Shannon enough that she had to be an older sister, wandered up with a ginger-haired toddler on her hip. The woman wore a modest, one-piece black swimsuit; the baby sported a swim diaper. She set him down and let him splash in the shallow water lapping at the hauled-in sand that made up the beach area. "Kyle, don't go too far out," she called to the boy on the float.

He waved impatiently at her and paddled harder while she turned her attention back to the baby.

Resting his head against the collapsible lounge chair he'd brought with him, James shifted his dark glasses on his nose and crossed his legs at the ankles. He wore navy swim trunks and a thin, pale gray T-shirt. His beach sandals sat on the brown sand beside the chair and a warm breeze tickled his bare feet. Considering it was an August Saturday afternoon, the heat wasn't too bad here by the waters of Greers Ferry Lake. He'd already had a long swim along the buoy line and had spent the past two hours resting, sipping bottled water and reading, though he'd brought a medical textbook rather than the usual beach read.

It had been pure impulse that made him toss the chair and a cooler of bottled water and sandwiches into his car and make the hour-long drive from his condo to the lake. A free Saturday was so rare in his schedule these days that he'd figured he had to do something to celebrate. He could have invited some of his friends to come with him, but he figured they were all busy on such short notice. His only friends these days were fellow medical students—specifically, the four other members of the study group he'd joined three years earlier.

He knew Anne's husband was in town and, since Liam traveled extensively, they would want to spend every spare minute together. Connor spent free weekends with his wife and almost-nine-year-old daughter. Newlyweds Haley and Ron were busily looking into residency programs in places that interested them both. Between those commitments and their hectic schedules as fourth-year medical students, none of them had much spare time. They were rarely able to take off on impulse.

He'd awakened that morning with a restless desire to get outside the confines of the hospital and his condo. The lake had been the first destination to pop into his head. He'd attended a class barbecue here in July, and he'd had such a nice time he decided to recapture the lazy good mood that day had inspired.

He quickly discovered it wasn't quite the same being here by himself. He'd had a pleasant day, but when he'd realized he was surrounded by families and groups of teenagers, he had become aware of his solitude. He was well accustomed to spending time alone and was content with his own company for the most part, but he supposed he'd become a bit spoiled by belonging to a tightly-knit group for the past three years— the first time in his almost thirty years he'd felt that close to anyone.

Maybe that was part of the reason he'd been so entertained watching the attractive Shannon and her family. Safely camouflaged behind the lenses of his dark glasses in his shady nook, he'd watched them play since they'd descended on the beach almost an hour earlier. At first he thought she might be the mother of some of the redheaded kids, but he'd since decided none of them were hers.

"Hey, Karen," she called to the woman with the book. "Tell my lazy brother to wake up and come play with us. Come on, Stu, get in the water."

The man dozing on the towel grumbled.

"Come swim with us, Daddy," the little boy Shannon had been tossing called out.

Stu sat up with exaggerated reluctance, stretching and yawning. At the water's edge, the toddler tripped and fell face-first into the wet sand, resulting in a wail that got everyone's attention. His mother righted him quickly, dusting off his chubby little legs and splashing water to divert him from his cries. "He's okay. Just startled him," she said.

Reassured, the others again started badgering Stu to join them in the water, everyone looking his way and laughing now.

James glanced idly past Shannon. Out by the buoys in the deeper water, the blue air mattress bobbed on the wake of a passing ski boat. Just as he straightened in his chair to look more closely, he saw a small red head emerge beside the floating mattress, then go beneath the water again, one hand flailing above the surface.

Tossing his sunglasses aside, he leaped from his chair. Dashing past the startled mother and toddler, he dived into the water just beyond where Shannon stood, striking out for the mattress with long, distance-eating strokes. He'd been out there earlier and he knew the water was a good twelve feet deep at the buoy line.

He heard someone scream behind him. Heard a woman yell, "Kyle!" Heard a splash and sensed someone following him through the choppy water, but his focus was on the empty float and the spot where he'd last seen the boy.

Drawing a deep breath, he ducked beneath the surface,

peering into the sediment-filled lake water and seeing nothing. He came back up for a quick gulp of air, then went back under, swinging his arms wide in hope of finding...

There. His fingers closed around wet skin. A flailing leg caught him in the stomach hard enough to make bubbles escape his mouth. Ignoring the pain, he grabbed hold of hair and skin and kicked upward, hauling the boy with him.

He gasped for air. Then released his breath in a sigh of relief when he heard the child in his grasp coughing and sputtering.

"Kyle!" Shannon swam up to them, her expression horrified. "Are you all right?"

The boy was trying not to cry, but not succeeding very well. "I fell off the float," he said, his words broken by racking coughs as James supported him. "I swallowed some water and I choked and I couldn't start swimming."

"Let's get him on the float and tow him in," James suggested, his arms still wrapped around the boy's chest as he treaded water for both of them.

Shannon nodded and looked toward the bank. "He's okay," she shouted toward the crowd that had gathered to watch anxiously from the beach. "We're bringing him in."

Bobbing in the water, she grabbed one end of the rubber float. "I'll steady this while you get him on it."

James nodded and looked at the boy, who had almost stopped coughing but began to look a little ill. "You'll be fine, Kyle," he assured him. "I'm going to hoist you onto your mattress, okay? Can you help steady yourself?"

Kyle nodded weakly. "I can swim," he muttered, clinging to what little pride he had left. "I just choked on some water."

"That happens sometimes," James replied matter-of-factly. "Okay, on three. One, two, three."

With the final count, he lifted the kid up and onto the mattress. While Shannon kept the float from tilting, Kyle grabbed the edges to keep his balance until it stopped rocking. Confident the boy wouldn't fall off again, James took hold of the rope attached to the top and struck out for the shore with Shannon swimming steadily on the other side of the mattress.

Leaving all the other kids on the shore, herded over by the woman who'd been reading earlier, Stu waded out to meet them as soon as their feet touched solid ground. Well, James's feet touched. Being several inches shorter, Shannon had to swim a little farther before she could stand.

"You okay, Kyle?" Stu asked the boy.

"I'm okay, Uncle Stu," Kyle murmured, looking both weary and mortified.

The mother of the toddler thrust her youngest child into the other woman's arms and dashed out to knee-deep water to clutch Kyle as Stu lifted him off the mattress. "You're okay, baby? You're sure you're okay?" she asked, patting him down as though looking for injuries.

"I'm okay," Kyle repeated, squirming. "Geez, Mom, don't call me 'baby' in front of everyone."

Now that her fears were somewhat relieved, fear turned to anger. "I told you not to go out that far. What were you thinking?" she scolded.

The boy's pouting lips were turning blue and he was beginning to shiver as his own emotional reactions flooded through him.

"You should probably get him out of the water and wrap him in a towel," James advised. "Don't want him to go into shock."

The calm advice brought everyone out of their panic-driven paralysis. Stu carried the boy to shore, where his mother grabbed a large, thick beach towel imprinted with cartoon superheroes and wrapped him snugly inside it. The non-related bystanders who'd gathered to gawk wandered back to their own pursuits, leaving the family gathered around Kyle.

"Kyle drownded," one of the younger kids said in awe.

"He didn't drown," Shannon said firmly. "He just came much too close."

Turning to James then, she gazed up at him with liquid green eyes. "I don't want to think about what might have happened if you hadn't been here. We thought we were watching them all so carefully."

The faint tug of familiarity nagged him again. *Had* he seen her somewhere before? She gave no sign of recognizing him.

"It's easy for kids to slip under the radar," he replied, thinking of the cases he'd seen in the emergency room when he'd done his pediatrics rotation last year. Many of the children brought in there had been injured when their adult supervisors had turned their backs only for a few moments.

Scooping her wet red hair away from her face, she grimaced. "We weren't careful enough," she said in self-recrimination. "Kyle really does swim well, and I guess we—I—thought he was okay on his float. I didn't realize he'd drifted so far out, or that he would fall off and be too startled to remember his swim training."

Drawing a deep, unsteady breath, she stuck out her dripping right hand. "I'm Shannon Gambill. Thank you for saving my nephew."

He wrapped his fingers around her hand. The feel of wet skin to wet skin was as pleasurable as it was somewhat unsettling. "James Stillman. It's nice to meet you, Shannon."

Shannon had been aware of the man watching her while she'd played with her nieces and nephews. Not in a creepy sort of way—and she had well-developed creep-dar. He looked like a man who was using a day off to do some rather heavy reading, judging from the size of the book he'd perused. Maybe just escaping from drudgery for a few hours. She liked to go off on her own sometimes to recharge her batteries and think in blessed solitude. She'd assumed he was doing something similar since he didn't seem to be accompanied by anyone.

Her older sister, Stacy, finally stopped hovering over Kyle to thank his rescuer. With typical exuberance, she threw her arms around James's middle, saying, "Thank you so much for saving my son. You're a true hero."

Shannon was rather amused by the "hero's" dumbstruck expression. It was obvious he wasn't accustomed to being embraced by tearful strangers. Somewhat awkwardly, he patted Stacy's shoulder, then carefully disentangled himself.

"Anyone would have done the same," he assured her in a self-conscious mumble. "I just happened to notice the boy was in trouble."

Her green eyes shining, Stacy shook her red head stubbornly and gazed up at him with an unsteady smile. "You were amazing. The way you just dived in and swam out there to save him… You should be given a medal or something."

James's cheeks were rather pink now. He glanced at Shannon as if begging for rescue, himself.

Smiling, she took pity on him, stepping forward to nudge her sister gently back a few inches. "This grateful mother is my sister, Stacy Malone. The twins are her oldest daughters, Briley and Baylee. You've met her son Kyle, of course, and the little one is Sammy."

Stacy reached out to clutch James's arm again. "I wish my husband, J.P., was here to thank you, too. He's working today, so he couldn't join us, but I know he'd want to express his gratitude for what you did for our family."

James cleared his throat. "Um—"

Pushing his emotional sister aside, Stu stepped up to take her place, extending his right hand to James. "Stu Gambill—Stacy and Shannon's older brother. It's nice to meet you, James."

Looking relieved by Stu's matter-of-fact tone, James shook his hand. "The pleasure is mine."

His rather old-fashioned phrasing matched the image Shannon was getting of him. She took pride in forming very accurate first impressions; it was almost a gift, as she'd bragged on more than one occasion. Maybe two or three years older than her own twenty-five years, he seemed very proper and scholarly, despite the muscles nicely defined by his wet T-shirt and swim trunks. Not shy, exactly, but reserved.

His hair was black, his eyes the color of rich, dark chocolate. His features were classically handsome—too masculine to be called "pretty," but definitely appealing. Not quite her type—even if he was extremely attractive—but he seemed nice, nonetheless.

Did he look just a little familiar? If so, she couldn't remember why.

Stu motioned to the woman at his side. "This is my wife, Karen. Our kids—Ginny, Jack and Caitlin. We're what you might call a prolific family," he added with a chuckle, waving toward the noisy cluster of siblings and cousins.

"Speak for yourself," Shannon murmured, drawing a glance from James.

"Can we go back in the water now?" Ginny asked, clutching her purple beach ball and edging toward the shoreline. Her cousin's misadventure was already consigned to a dramatic memory.

Kyle's teeth had stopped chattering and Shannon was relieved to see his color was almost back to normal. The freckles across his cheeks no longer stood out as dramatically as they had when he'd been pulled from the water, pale and panic-stricken. She wouldn't forget that look for a while, she thought with a hard swallow.

"I want to swim, too," Kyle insisted, squirming out of the towel his mother had wrapped so tightly around him he could hardly move. Shannon suspected he wanted to prove to everyone that his near-drowning hadn't made him afraid to go back in the water. Kyle's innate recklessness was the bane of his harried mother's existence.

"No more swimming right now," Stu proclaimed. "It's almost time to eat," he added, raising his voice slightly to be heard over the chorus of protests. "I bet Grandpa and Uncle Lou have already got the coals heating back at the picnic area."

"And don't forget we're having homemade ice cream for dessert," Karen reminded them.

That was enough to divert the kids' attention from water sports. They snatched up towels, toys and shoes in preparation to return to the picnic area.

"Are you by yourself today?" Shannon asked James.

He nodded. "Rare day off. It seemed like a good time to swim and read."

Exactly as she'd surmised, she thought smugly. "My family's having a cookout. We always have enough food for at least a dozen extra people. We would love to have you join us for burgers and ice cream."

He looked startled again by the impulsive invitation, but Stacy jumped on the suggestion immediately. "Oh, yes, please do, James. Our parents would love to meet you."

"Oh, but I—"

"Our family's a little crazy, but a fun bunch," Stu chimed in. "If you don't mind sharing burgers with a few bees and a gang of rug rats, you'd be welcome."

"No bees," eight-year-old Ginny announced confidently. "Grandpa brought Cinderella candles."

"Citronella," Karen corrected her daughter with a smothered smile.

"I wouldn't want to intrude," James said.

Studying his face, Shannon thought he looked tempted by the invitation, even though he seemed to feel obliged to demur. That was all the impetus she needed to smile up at him and urge, "It wouldn't be an intrusion at all. Our family loves making new friends. And after what you've done for us, we consider you a friend already."

He pushed a hand through his wet, black hair, his dark eyes steady on her face. "Then I would be pleased to accept. On one condition. You have to stop thanking me. I was happy to be of assistance, but any of you would have done the same thing if you'd seen a boy in trouble."

She laughed. "Well, you'll probably have to endure my parents' expressions of gratitude when they hear the story, but after that I promise we'll drop the hero treatment, if you like."

"I'd like," he agreed with a faint smile.

She stuck out her hand. "Deal."

His eyes glinting with amusement, he shook her hand again. Once again, she was aware of an odd tingling when they made skin-to-skin contact. She'd thought that was only an anomaly the first time. No surprise, really, she assured herself. After all, the guy was good-looking. And his long-lashed eyes were striking enough to make a healthy young woman's heart flutter a little.

She was a healthy young woman.

His fingers tightened for only a moment around hers—as if she weren't the only one aware of a spark between them—but then he released her and stepped back, his expression politely neutral again. "I'll get my things."

The others went ahead toward the picnic area, the three adults shepherding the seven children up the asphalt road, a task Shannon silently compared to herding cats. Slipping her feet into her sandals, she drew a loose, thin, white cover-up over her bikini. The sleeveless, thigh-length garment clung a bit to her damp suit, but it was cool, comfortable and modest enough to satisfy her mother and aunt.

She towel-dried her collar-length curls while James donned his sandals, draped a towel around the neck of his wet T-shirt and folded his chair. He tucked the chair beneath one arm, then picked up the small cooler and thick book that had been sitting beside it.

"I'll drop these things off at my car," he said. "It's parked at the edge of the day area. I have some dry clothing in the car. I'd like to change before eating."

"Of course. The changing rooms aren't far from the tables we've claimed." Imitating him, she looped her towel around her neck to free her hands. "Can I help you carry something?"

"That's not necessary. I've—"

But she had already relieved him of the heavy hardcover tome as she fell into step beside him toward the parking lot. She discovered in surprise that it was a medical reference book. *"Textbook of Infectious Diseases?"* she asked in surprise. "Holy kamoley. You consider this beach reading?"

Amused by her wording, he shrugged. "It's the only thing I have time to read at the moment."

"You're a doctor?"

"Medical student," he corrected her. "Just started my fourth year."

"Oh." She wouldn't have been surprised had he said he was a doctor, because she'd pegged him as a professional man from the start, but she hadn't expected him to still be in school. "Is medical school as tough as everyone says?"

"It's challenging," he said neutrally.

She would be willing to bet he was at the top of his class, and that the material came more easily to him than to others. He had an air of quiet competence that made her think he didn't often fail at anything he attempted. She'd bet he was the single-minded, long-term-planning, never-give-up type, too.

She watched as he placed his folding chair into the backseat of a sleek, expensive hybrid car and drew out a small, designer-label duffel bag. Money, she decided immediately. A social conscience, but no worries about paying his bills. Privileged background—private schools? Lifelong country-club membership? Social-register girlfriends?

Okay, maybe she was getting a little carried away with her predilection for making sweeping assumptions based on early impressions, she decided, reining in her imaginings. Her family had warned her she was going to be disappointed or even hurt someday when one of her first impressions turned out to be way off the mark. But because she believed at least most of her guesses about James were close to reality that meant they couldn't be less suited. She kept her smile friendly rather than flirty when she handed him his textbook and told him she would meet him at the picnic area after he'd changed into his dry clothes.

James needn't have worried about finding Shannon's family after he changed into a green polo shirt and khaki cargo shorts. He spotted the clan as soon as he walked into the day-use area of the surrounding wooded campgrounds. They had claimed two picnic tables and a charcoal grill, from which smoke was streaming.

It was immediately obvious that he was expected. As soon as he appeared, a woman who looked like an older, blonde version of Shannon and Stacy dashed forward to greet him, holding out both hands in welcome. She caught his hands in hers, squeezing as though she would really prefer to be hugging him, the way Stacy had earlier. "Thank you so much for saving my grandson. Our family owes you such a huge debt of gratitude."

He'd braced himself for this, but it didn't make it any easier. He wasn't at all comfortable being treated like a hero just for doing what anyone else would have done under the circumstances. For that matter, one of the other adults would probably have seen Kyle's predicament only a moment or two after James had. He was just glad he'd been able to help.

"Okay, Mom, you've embarrassed James enough," Shannon said, fondly nudging her mother back a few inches. "Let Dad thank him and then we're going to cut the man some slack and let him eat a burger in peace."

A man with a ring of hair that might once have been red circling a glossy bald head stepped forward to offer a hand to James. "Hollis Gambill. Consider yourself thanked again."

The man's calm, but sincere tone reminded James of Stu. "It's a pleasure to meet you, sir."

"Call me Hollis. You answer to James or Jim?"

"Either, but I generally prefer James."

Hollis nodded, apparently making a mental note of the preference as he motioned toward the people crowding around him. "This is my wife, Virginia. And my brother, Lou, and his wife, Lois."

Hands were shaken all around and then James was towed toward the picnic tables, where the adults he'd met at the swimming area were all either cooking, setting out supplies for dinner, or supervising the seven children making noisy use of the nearby playground equipment. Stacy was one of the supervisors and she barely took her eyes off Kyle. James suspected that young man's adventures were going to be closely monitored for the foreseeable future.

He offered his assistance with the dinner preparations, but was assured everything was under control. "Shannon, get your guest something cold to drink," her mother ordered. "The food will be ready in just a minute."

"*Our* guest, Mom," Shannon corrected in a murmur. "What would you like, James? We have beer, bottled water, diet cola, fruit juices…."

He interrupted with a chuckle. "Bottled water will be fine. Thanks."

She handed him a plastic bottle with a teasing, "Here you go, Doc."

"Doc?" Her aunt Lois set down a stack of paper plates and studied James from the other side of the concrete picnic table where he'd been urged to have a seat. "You're a doctor?"

"A medical student," he corrected. "Fourth year."

She waved a hand dismissively. "Can you write me a prescription for those little yellow pills that perk me up when I'm feeling peckish? My doctor at home is being a real fuddy-duddy and he won't let me have any more, but I told him I don't overuse them. I just like to have them around when I need them."

Though he'd been warned it could happen, it was the first time he'd actually been hit up for a prescription. "I'm afraid I can't do that, Mrs. Gambill. As a medical student, I'm not allowed to write prescriptions."

"Honestly, Lois," Shannon's mother scolded her sister-in-law. "This nice young man is going to think you're a druggy. Don't go pestering him for pills."

"But I—"

"I'm sorry if Lois put you on the spot," Virginia continued to James, ignoring Lois's protests. "She isn't really a drug addict."

He struggled against a smile. "I didn't think so."

Virginia turned then to her daughter-in-law. "Karen, you should have the doctor look at that rash on Caitlin's back and tummy. Maybe he'd know what's causing it."

"I'm not a doctor yet," he reiterated. "I'm a medical student."

"Bet you've seen a few rashes, though, haven't you?"

"Well, I—"

"Caitlin. Come see Grammy, sweetie."

"But I—"

"We did warn you the family's crazy," Shannon murmured, standing close behind him and not even bothering to hide a wry grin.

Because he wasn't sure what to say in response to that, he didn't even try. Little Caitlin, the five-year-old with hair that glowed almost neon orange, dutifully lifted her shirt upon her grandmother's instructions, baring her tummy to James's reluctant eyes. A blotchy pink rash splashed her skin, extending to her back when she turned around. James was relieved when they merely told him it was also on her bottom, rather than stripping her down to prove it.

"It doesn't really look like heat rash to me," Shannon's mother fretted. "And it's definitely not measles or chicken pox, because she's had her vaccinations. I know what they look like, anyway. What do you think?"

"Probably not heat rash," James agreed, trying to recall his days in the outpatient peds clinic. "It looks like contact dermatitis to me. Have you changed laundry detergents lately?"

"No," Karen replied, straightening her daughter's clothes. "I've used the same one since she was born."

"I noticed the rash is only where her clothing touches," he explained.

Everyone looked at the child, nodding to agree with his comment.

"Actually, Stu's been doing the laundry this week," Karen said thoughtfully, looking toward her husband. "I've been busy with other things. Stu?"

Turning from the smoking grill, her husband asked, "You need something, honey?"

"You've been using the regular laundry detergent this week, haven't you?"

"Sure. Same kind we've always used," he replied.

Virginia sighed in disappointment that their guest had been proven wrong.

"It was only a guess," James said with a slight shrug. "I'm afraid I don't know what's causing the—"

"I did change fabric softeners, though," Stu called out. "We ran out and another brand was on sale. Smelled good, so I thought I'd try it."

Virginia beamed at James. "Well, there you go. She's allergic to the fabric softener."

"A sensitivity to it, perhaps. Probably not a true allergy," he said.

Caitlin had already dashed off to play with her siblings and cousins again, her fun unimpeded by the rash that had concerned the adults.

"That was very clever of you," Lois said to James, patting his shoulder approvingly. "Are you sure you can't prescribe my little pills?"

"I'm sure, Mrs. Gambill."

"Oh, call her Lois," Virginia ordered. "And I'm Virginia. If you say Mrs. Gambill, Lois and Karen and I are all likely to answer."

"Meat's ready," Hollis announced, setting a huge tray of steaming burgers and franks in the center of the table. "Stacy, you and Karen go ahead and fix the kids' plates and let them start eating so the rest of us can enjoy our dinners."

"Sit by your guest, Shannon," her mother ordered, motioning toward the bench beside James. "You're in the way here."

Shannon heaved a sigh and moved to slide onto the bench

beside him. "You're in for it now," she warned him in a low voice, her smile both mischievous and contagious. "Not only are you the hero who saved my nephew, you're a doctor. I should warn you that the whole family will try to fix us up during the meal."

"Fix us up?" he repeated.

"Yeah. They've been trying for months to match me up with someone. After all, I had my twenty-fifth birthday last spring, and I'm single and unattached—which, you can probably tell, is unheard of in this family of early breeders. You must look like a prize stud to them."

Her blunt phrasing took him aback for a moment, but then she laughed. Her green eyes sparkled with humor and her grin was an invitation to share a secret joke with her.

It was an offer he couldn't resist. He laughed, too, earning them approving smiles from Shannon's mother and aunt. This, of course, only made them laugh harder.

James couldn't actually remember the last time he'd laughed out loud like this. It felt pretty damned good, he decided, still smiling when he turned to the heaping plate of food his hosts nudged encouragingly toward him.

Chapter Two

It was, to say the least, an interesting meal. The Gambill clan was as colorful as their hair. They talked a lot, and everyone at once, so it was sometimes hard to follow all the conversations going on around him. He tried to keep them all straight—the men talked about baseball, Karen and Stacy chatted about their kids, Virginia and Lois seemed determined to learn everything there was to know about James, Shannon kept up a running beneath-her-breath commentary, and the kids interrupted every few moments with requests, tattling and other bids for attention.

"What type of medicine do you want to practice, James?" Virginia asked, cutting off a sports comment from her husband.

"I'm considering pediatric infectious disease, though I find pulmonology intriguing, too."

He saw no need to mention that he had a younger cousin with cystic fibrosis, which perhaps explained his interest in pulmonology. Watching Kelly's lifelong battle with the disease and hearing about the excellent care she had received from the doctors at the children's hospital had probably been part of what had influenced him to enter medical school after receiving his advanced science degree, despite his parents' displeasure that he'd chosen to leave academia. His parents were more interested in theory than practice in almost all disciplines, expounding that the true geniuses developed science while those of lesser intelligence and imagination put it to everyday use.

"Lou has a touch of emphysema," Lois said eagerly, drawing James's thoughts away from his parents' affectations. "Maybe you could listen to his lungs later."

"I'm afraid I don't have a stethoscope with me," he replied.

Virginia rolled her eyes. "Honestly, Lois. You've been after poor James for free prescriptions and exams ever since you found out he's a medical student."

Lois huffed. "Aren't you the one who asked him to look at your granddaughter's rash?"

"That's different. I was simply asking for an opinion, not drugs."

"I didn't ask him to prescribe anything for Lou. I just thought he might want to listen."

"Why would he want to do that?" Virginia demanded with a shake of her head.

"They've been arguing like that for more than sixty years," Shannon informed James quietly, leaning toward him so he could hear her better over the noise of all the others. Her shoulder brushed his as they sat side by side on the bench.

A bit too keenly aware of that point of contact, he tried to concentrate on what she had said. "So they knew each other before they married brothers."

"They're first cousins. They were raised almost like sisters. Makes the family tree a little complicated."

"I see. And you all live in this area?"

"I live in Little Rock, and so do Stu and Karen. Stacy and J.P. live in Bryant. Uncle Lou and Aunt Lois are visiting from St. Louis and staying for a few days with my parents in Sherwood. They have two daughters and five grandchildren of their own back in Missouri. Needless to say, it's pretty crazy when both families get together on occasion."

"Are you from this area, James?" Virginia asked.

Swallowing a bite of his juicy, perfectly grilled burger, James wiped his mouth on a paper napkin before replying. "I'm from northwest Arkansas. Fayetteville. My parents moved there from Tennessee when I was twelve. They're both professors at the university."

"Got my degree there," Stu commented as he scooped potato salad onto a plastic fork. "Karen and I met at a music club on Dickson Street when I was a senior and she was a junior."

"You'd have been a student there after Stu and Karen," Lois commented, looking James over assessingly. "Stu's thirty-eight. You're—what—thirty?"

"I will be on October fifth. But I didn't get my degree at Fayetteville. I went to Vanderbilt."

Several of the people around him frowned and he could tell he'd just lost a few Arkie points.

"I'm still a Razorbacks fan, though," he assured them. "Uh—woo, Pigs."

The frowns turned to chuckles and conversation moved to the prospects for the next SEC football season.

"Nice save," Shannon murmured into his ear. "Do you even like football?"

"Couldn't care less," he replied from behind his burger.

She laughed. "That's what I thought."

A noisy argument erupted from the kids' table, requiring adult intervention, and then the overlapping conversations moved to new topics. During the next twenty minutes, James learned that Hollis was a retired quality-control manager, Virginia had been a dental hygienist, Stu was an elementary school principal, Karen an accounting office manager and Stacy was a stay-at-home mom married to a police officer.

"You haven't mentioned what you do," he commented to Shannon when there was a momentary lull in the chatter.

"Shannon drifts," Stacy murmured, hearing the question.

Virginia seemed both annoyed and mildly alarmed by that remark. She looked at James as if worried he'd take Stacy's comment the wrong way. "Shannon is so good at everything that she has a hard time narrowing her interests down to one career."

Shannon grinned. "Yeah, that's it. I'm too good to pin down."

Her mother frowned at her.

Ignoring the silent censure, Shannon looked at James again. "I've had a few jobs that didn't work out. You might say I get restless easily. But I just started a new business and I like it quite a bit."

"What's your new business?"

"I'm running a kids' party business. I call it Kid Capers. Birthday parties mostly, though I do an occasional tea party or other special-occasion event. I handle all the planning and make the arrangements so all the parents have to do is show up and write a check afterward. It's fun."

"I see. Is there a big demand for kids' party planners?" he asked, genuinely curious.

She shrugged. "The struggling economy isn't helping, but there are still quite a few people who are willing to pay to have someone else take care of all the party details."

"I'm surprised you're free on a Saturday afternoon. Did you leave this day open to spend time with your family?"

"I, um, didn't have any bookings today," she admitted. "Like I said, a lot of people are pinching pennies these days."

"Shannon really does throw some amazing parties," her mother said loyally. "She has a binder full of themes for the clients to choose from or she takes their ideas and makes them work. She's young, of course, and just getting started, but we've all offered to assist her in any way we can."

"And as much as I appreciate the offer, I've told you repeatedly that I've got everything under control," Shannon said with a firmness that made James suspect there had been a few arguments about that subject.

"By working part-time at a toy store to pay her bills," Stacy murmured.

"Just twenty-five hours a week," Shannon said quickly. "The manager there is very good to let me keep my weekends free for my new business and I enjoy working at the toy store. For one thing, it keeps me current on what's popular with the kids for party themes."

Shannon's father chuckled. "I keep telling Shannon these fancy parties for kids are just downright frivolous. Back when our kids were little, we had cake and ice cream and a bunch of neighborhood pals over for pin-the-tail-on-the-donkey and Twister. That was the extent of it."

"Mama hired a pony for my birthday once, remember, Hollis?" his brother, Lou, reminisced. "My tenth, I think. I still remember how much fun that was."

"And she didn't need a planner to help her with it," Hollis said pointedly.

Shannon tilted her head at him. "Okay, Dad. We got your point."

She didn't sound cross, exactly, James decided, studying the family dynamics. More resigned and just a little irked, as if she were used to her family indulgently dismissing her work—rather as if she didn't like it, but half expected it, anyway.

"Do you remember a special birthday party from your youth, James?" Lois asked, looking eager to jump into the conversation again.

"I never actually had a birthday party. My parents weren't really into that sort of thing."

The sudden silence around the table was rather jarring after so much chatter.

"You never had a birthday party?" Virginia asked. "Surely you had a few friends over for cake."

"Well, no. But my parents always took me to a nice restaurant on my birthday." Uncomfortable with that conversational direction, he picked up the last segment of his sandwich. "This hamburger is delicious. What seasonings did you use, Hollis?"

"That's a family secret," Hollis replied with a grin. "We don't share it with anyone who isn't born a Gambill or married into the family."

"It's Cajun seasoning and Worcestershire sauce," Shannon said with a roll of her eyes. "So, you can make your own hamburgers without proposing to anyone here."

"Now you've done it, Shannon," Stu scolded her with mock outrage. "Now we have to kill him."

"Stu's only joking, of course, James," Lois said in a stage whisper.

He smiled. "Yes, ma'am. I know."

"When do we get the ice cream, Mama?" one of the twins called out.

Hollis climbed out from behind the picnic table. "The ice cream is ready. Who wants strawberry and who wants peach?"

"Strawberry!"

"Peach!"

"Chocolate!"

Karen sighed. "We don't have any chocolate, Jack. You'll get peach."

The kids went crazy when the rich homemade ice cream was spooned out of the stainless-steel tubs. The adults attacked the dessert with almost as much enthusiasm. James accepted a bowl of strawberry ice cream, which he enjoyed very much.

Shannon jumped a couple of feet when one of her little nieces dropped a scoop of strawberry ice cream down the front of her top.

"Holy kamoley, that's cold!" she said, her voice suspiciously high-pitched as she snatched frantically for paper napkins. Rather than helping, her family laughed heartlessly as she did a funny dance trying to swipe the sticky, ice-cold mixture from her skin.

"Since she started her kids' party business, Shannon's taken to saying *holy kamoley* in place of any curse words," Stacy explained to James with an indulgent, big-sister smile. "It's rather annoying, but we're getting used to it."

He thought it was sort of funny, himself. Never having had an older sibling—or a younger one, for that matter—he wondered if Shannon minded being treated like one of the little kids dashing around the tables.

It was an interesting family, he mused, continuing to study them as they finished the dessert. Noisy, freewheeling, outspoken, good-humored, they gabbed and joked and argued and teased. So very different from his own family. He wondered what it would have been like to grow up in a family like this one, how he might have turned out.

An argument erupted among some of the children, and though it was dealt with quickly and firmly, everyone had to laugh when little Sammy piped in with a gusty, "Holy 'moley!"

James grinned, thinking how much his friend Ron would enjoy hearing about this eccentric clan. Ron usually had a funny anecdote to share when the study group managed to get together these days; next time, James would have a story of his own.

"Can we go swimming again?" one of the kids asked when the ice cream bowls had been scraped clean.

"No more swimming today," Stacy said firmly. "But we can play ball. We brought the plastic bats and balls and the little rubber bases and there's plenty of room on the grass over there to play."

"Will Uncle Stu be the pitcher?"

Stu nodded. "Gladly. Aunt Shannon can be the catcher."

"We don't actually form teams," Shannon explained to James. "We just let each kid bat and run the bases. That keeps them entertained for a while."

"Sounds like fun."

"Want to join us? You can play shortstop. Aunt Lois tends to get distracted and wander off during the game."

He chuckled, but shook his head. "Thanks, but I'd better head back to Little Rock. I have to be at the hospital early in the morning."

The entire family protested when he announced he was leaving. He shook hands with the men again, waved off another round of thanks for his rescue of young Kyle, accepted hugs and cheek kisses from the women—and was less surprised when they were offered this time, since he'd gotten a bit more familiar with their demonstrativeness.

Lois insisted on giving him a handful of homemade oatmeal raisin cookies wrapped in a paper napkin. She told him she intended to bring them out after the ball game, in case anyone could possibly still be hungry by then.

"Thank you," he said. "I'll enjoy these."

"Good. I hope to see you again sometime," she replied. Tugging at his arm to get him to bend closer to her, she whispered, "My niece is single, you know."

He smothered a smile and evaded the comment by saying, "It was very nice to meet you, Lois."

"Shannon, why don't you walk James to his car?" Virginia suggested.

He supposed he should have insisted he didn't need an escort, but he figured he'd be wasting his breath. Not to mention that he didn't mind spending a little more time with Shannon, even if only to walk to his car.

Once again he couldn't quite tell what she was thinking when she nodded in response to her mother's hint and turned to walk with him. Maybe she was simply thinking along the same lines as he—that it would be useless to protest. Not particularly flattering, if that were true.

He let her walk a couple of steps ahead of him toward the parking lot. Her thin white cover-up fluttered when she walked, floating around her slender body to end at midthigh. He could just see the outline of her yellow bikini through the now-dry fabric. Her hair had dried into a mop of soft red curls that looked temptingly touchable.

When she glanced back at him with a smile, it occurred to him that she wore no makeup, but she didn't need enhancement. He found the splash of golden freckles across her nose and cheeks intriguing and couldn't imagine why she would want to hide them. While she probably wouldn't be described as a true beauty, he couldn't imagine anything he would change about her fresh, pretty features.

He realized abruptly that he didn't want to tell her goodbye and drive away without any prospect of seeing her again.

James cleared his throat as they reached his car, and Shannon braced herself, wishing they could skip past what she sensed was coming. She had hoped he would be immune to her relatives' heavy-handed hints.

"I enjoyed the meal with your family," he said, giving her one of his intriguingly faint smiles. "Thank you for inviting me to join you."

"The least we could do," she assured him. "And everyone enjoyed meeting you."

She hoped that sounded casual and generic enough.

He frowned just a little, as if it had indeed caught his attention that she hadn't referred specifically to herself, but he smoothed the expression almost immediately. "I'd like to hear more about your business sometime. It sounds very interesting."

"You should check my Web site. Kid Capers dot com. All the details are there."

His frown lasted a bit longer this time. "Um, yeah, I'll check that out. But what I meant was, I'd like to hear more from you. Maybe we could have dinner sometime?"

He really was an attractive man. His dark hair was so thick and temptingly touchable. His elusive smile made her want to go to extra lengths to earn it. She liked the way he moved—with a deliberateness that was both elegant and masculine all at the same time. Her prided instincts told her this man was actually a study in contrasts—cordial, yet reserved; friendly, yet private; open to others, yet somehow closed on a personal level.

It was the latter quality that made her smile regretfully and shake her head. "I'm afraid I'm very busy right now, between my part-time job and getting my new business off the ground. I know you're quite busy, too, so perhaps it would be best if we just say goodbye. It was very nice meeting you, James."

His expression unreadable, he nodded and shook the hand she offered him. She tried without much success to ignore the frisson of awareness that went through her again when their palms touched so briefly. There were most definitely sparks here, she thought, rather quickly pulling away. Which didn't mean she should place herself in a position to get burned. She still bore the scars from the last time she'd played with fire, romantically speaking.

"Goodbye, Shannon. Enjoy your ball game."

With that, he climbed into his car. She turned to rejoin her family, but couldn't resist glancing over her shoulder as he drove away. She was aware of a funny little pang inside her when the car disappeared from her sight. Ordering herself to get over it, she drew a deep breath in preparation for her family's scolding for letting that nice young doctor slip away.

Shannon hung up her cell phone with a satisfied smile. "And it's a deal," she murmured, pumping her fist in a gesture of success.

Devin Caswell, her friend, housemate and occasional assistant, clapped her hands with a muted cheer. "You got the gig?"

"Booked it."

"Details?"

Shannon glanced at her notes. "Birthday party, nine-year-old girl, first Saturday in September—two weeks from tomorrow—at the home. The kid takes dance lessons, plays soccer, loves purple, like every other nine-year-old girl in the world and enjoys handcrafts. Her mom wants each guest to leave the party with a hand-crafted item to keep as a favor. I suggested decorated tote bags or headbands or beaded necklaces or friendship bracelets. She liked them all."

Devin chuckled. "Going to be interesting trying to work all of that into a two-hour party."

Wrinkling her nose, Shannon made another note on the pad. "The mom gave me free rein to come up with the projects, though I have a somewhat limited budget. It won't be a big bash, but I'll still make a small profit and that's what counts. Maybe I'll get some more jobs out of it."

"Two weeks. Short notice, wasn't it?"

"She apologized for that. She said she had intended to handle all the arrangements herself, but apparently she's realized she just doesn't have time to do the party justice. She said a friend of her husband's recommended me. She was vague about who it was; I assume it was a former client. I'll ask again next time I talk to her, so I can thank whoever it was for the referral."

With a wry smile, she added, "Mrs. Hayes seemed to think it was a miracle we didn't already have a party scheduled that day. I didn't bother to mention we're more likely to be free than booked on any given Saturday."

Dark-haired, dark-eyed Devin wagged a finger, trying to keep her expression stern rather than amused. "Of course you didn't mention that. One has to look successful to be successful, right?"

"Exactly." That was the reason she and Devin had set up the living room of their small, rented house with as much an eye toward hosting potential clients as entertaining friends. The TV was housed in a cabinet with a door they kept closed when not in use. Few knickknacks cluttered the polished surfaces of the tables on either end of the plain, beige couch accessorized with a few colorful throw pillows. The framed posters on the walls were inexpensive, but tasteful.

Bookcases grouped around a round wood table in one corner of the room held albums of photographs and sample materials for the theme parties. The clutter of bookkeeping, order forms and supplies was stashed in the bedrooms and the tiny, barely-one-car garage used only for storage.

She hadn't needed to show Mia Hayes any of the samples, she mused, glancing at the telephone. Mrs. Hayes had asked only a few questions before booking Shannon's services. Whoever had passed along the recommendation must have been convincing. Shannon made a mental note to try to find out who it had been. Word of mouth was invaluable in this budding business and she wanted to make sure to express her gratitude.

She glanced at her watch, realizing she would have to try to solve that mystery later. "I'd better get going. Don't want to be late to work."

Having spent most of the last night at the hospital where she worked as a Certified Nurse Assistant, Devin yawned and nodded. "I'm headed to bed for a few hours. By the way, when you get home, I want to ask you about someone you met recently. A handsome young doctor?"

Freezing in the process of reaching for her purse, Shannon looked over her shoulder as a vividly clear image of James Stillman popped into her head. Six days had passed since their meeting at the lake, but she still had no trouble recalling every detail of his appearance. She could even still hear his deep, pleasant voice echoing in her ears as he'd asked her to dinner.

"How did you hear about that?"

"Talked to Stacy before work last night. She mentioned him, then asked if I knew him from the hospital. I told her the name doesn't sound familiar. I don't know all the med students, of course, only the ones working in post-op during my hours."

Shannon sighed lightly. Stacy had probably given a dramatically embellished account of her son's rescue. Who knew what else she'd said?

"Kyle fell off his floating mattress and a nice medical student happened to be there to help him. One of us probably would have noticed and gotten to him in time, but we were very grateful to James for his assistance. We asked him to join us for burgers, he did, it was all very pleasant and then he left. End of story."

"Hmm." Devin eyed her assessingly. "How come you didn't tell me about that before? How come *you* didn't ask if I knew him?"

Shannon still wasn't sure why she hadn't described the incident to Devin. Maybe because she was still chagrined she and her siblings had been so momentarily lax with watching the kids in the water. She didn't even want to think about the worst-case outcome of that negligence.

As for the meeting with James, it was a onetime thing, so hardly worth mentioning. Right? "It didn't come up. We've both been so busy lately."

"Stacy said the guy sure seemed taken with you. Did he ask for your number?"

"No, he didn't." She wasn't lying, she assured herself. Devin hadn't inquired if James had asked her out.

Her housemate frowned in disapproval. "And you didn't offer it?"

"I did not. I didn't even know the guy."

"According to Stacy, he was a gorgeous doctor-to-be who rescued your nephew and was nice to your aging relatives. What more do you need to know?"

Devin had fallen into the habit of serving as surrogate big sister to Shannon when Stacy wasn't around. She'd been known to fuss about Shannon's not-always-healthy eating habits, about her not always getting enough sleep or working too hard at her two jobs. Shannon didn't like being supervised by her housemate any more than she did by her family. She had learned to be very firm in drawing boundaries with Devin.

Tucking her purse beneath her arm, she reached determinedly for her car keys. "I'm leaving now. Get some sleep, Dev."

Looking dissatisfied, Devin sighed. "Okay, fine. See you later."

Shannon opened the front door. "See you."

Thoughts of James Stillman drifted through her mind as she made the drive to the west Little Rock toy store where she worked part-time. If she were being honest, she would have to admit it hadn't taken the reminder from her housemate to bring him to her mind. Images of him had popped into her head too many times since their encounter.

He was the first man who'd seriously caught her attention in several months, but she wasn't convinced she'd been wrong to turn down his invitation. Something inside her had warned that even a simple dinner date with James could lead to complications. Ever since her last painful relationship—the second romantic disaster in her relatively short life—she'd vowed to herself to always listen to her instincts from that point on.

She had just finished assisting a customer with finding a popular doll accessory two hours later when her sixth sense, or whatever it was, kicked into overdrive again. Blinking in a startled reaction to the sudden, unusual tingling feeling, she turned warily.

Looking preppy and gorgeous in a dark blue polo shirt and crisply pressed khaki pants, James Stillman smiled at her from the end of the aisle. "Hello, Shannon."

Caught off guard by seeing him there—and by the presentiment that had been odd even for her—she gaped at him a moment before regaining her composure. "James. What are you doing here?"

Chapter Three

If James heard any suspicion in her question, it didn't show in his easy smile. "I'm here to buy a gift for a friend's daughter. Maybe you could help me choose something? To be honest, I'm clueless when it comes to that sort of thing."

She eyed him with a frown. Was he really here only to buy a gift? He had just happened to come to the store where she worked for the purchase? She was pretty sure he'd heard the name of the store at the picnic. Had he come here today because she might be here, or was that speculation just conceit on her part?

The store manager, Bill Travis, walked by just in time to hear James's comment. He smiled at the potential customer, then glanced at Shannon as if wondering what was taking her so long to reply. "She'll be glad to help you, sir. Don't hesitate to ask Shannon for any assistance you need."

James nodded at the passing manager. "Thanks."

Bill shot another look at Shannon, then continued on toward

the back of the store where the offices and storage rooms were located.

Switching to the briskly professional tone she used with all the store's customers, Shannon gave James a bright smile. "I'd be delighted to assist you. How old is your friend's daughter?"

"Alexis is turning nine in a couple of weeks. What sort of thing do nine-year-old girls like?"

The girl's name, along with her age, made a lightbulb turn on in Shannon's head. "This girl's last name wouldn't be Hayes, would it?"

He lifted his dark eyebrows in surprise. "Why, yes. Alexis Hayes. How did you know?"

She sighed, uncertain herself how she'd put those particular dots together so quickly. "Her mother called me this morning to handle the birthday party arrangements. She said she'd been given my name by a friend. That would be you, wouldn't it?"

"It would. Her husband, my friend and classmate, Connor, mentioned that Mia was really snowed under with her grad-school work, teaching duties and their daughter's activities. He can't help her much right now because he's on a difficult rotation. When he said they were trying to find time to arrange a birthday party for Alexis, I suggested they contact you. Mia liked the idea of having someone else do all the work and planning for once."

"Oh." She wasn't sure how she felt about acquiring the job through James. It was her nature as the often patronizingly-indulged youngest sibling to immediately resist whenever it seemed that someone was offering her a handout, as if she were some charity case who needed assistance handling her own affairs. Her prickly independence, as Philip had referred to it, had been a definite sore spot between them.

But then she told herself she should be happy for any

booking, no matter how it had come about, and chided herself for being unreasonable. Hadn't she been grateful earlier for the word-of-mouth business? Before she'd learned from whose mouth the advice had issued? "Thank you. I appreciate the referral. I'll do a good job for your friend."

He smiled. "I wouldn't have recommended you if I'd thought otherwise."

There it was again. That faint, somewhat elusive tilt of his lips that made her heart flutter foolishly and her own mouth tingle as if in wistful anticipation.

Turning brusquely toward the shelves of dolls and accessories, she spoke in a deliberately businesslike manner. "These things are probably too young for a nine-year-old. How well do you know Alexis?"

"I've known her since she was six, but that doesn't mean I know what sort of things she likes," he admitted. "She's a cute kid. Smart. Polite. Active. That's about the sum of what I can tell you."

"Her mother said she likes dance and soccer and the color purple."

"Sounds like her. You get any ideas for gifts out of that?"

"She also likes handcrafts." She led him to another aisle filled with handcraft kits. "These are designed for children her age."

James studied rows of kits for making stuffed toys and jewelry and sun catchers and hair accessories. Nothing seemed to interest him much. "I don't know."

"Okay, let's look at this section," she said, stepping around him. Their arms brushed as she did so and she was annoyed that her pulse rate stuttered in response to the contact. Focusing fiercely on the job at hand, she pointed out several rows of art supplies. "Does she like to draw or paint?"

"Actually, I have seen several pictures she drew displayed

on the fridge when I've studied at their house," he replied thoughtfully. "She's pretty good, for a kid."

"Maybe a box of pastels," she suggested, picking up a small but nice set. He hadn't said what he wanted to spend, but she figured that was a safe guess.

James examined the pastels she handed him, but his attention was quickly drawn to a larger art-supplies set packaged in a wooden box with brass hinges on each side. The box opened from the center to reveal a rainbow selection of colored pencils, pastels, watercolors and tubes of oil paints, graphite drawing pencils, erasers, sharpeners and other supplies.

Recommended for ages eight and up, the set was rather pricey—more than Shannon would be able to spend on her nieces and nephews for birthday gifts. She noted that James didn't even check the price.

"This looks nice. Maybe she'd like this."

"Any kid who likes to draw and paint would love that set. Heck, I'd like it, myself," she added with a grin.

She was being quite candid. She had loved drawing and painting since her own childhood, though she considered herself only marginally talented. Artistic enough to come in handy for her children's parties, anyway. Unfortunately, this lovely set was out of her miscellaneous-expense budget.

"Okay, I'll get this," James announced in sudden decision. "If she doesn't care for it, I assume she can exchange it for something else?"

"Of course she can. But I bet she'll keep it."

She remembered her impression that James came from a privileged background. He certainly didn't fit the image of a financially struggling medical student. But she didn't get the feeling he was flashing his money, either. He seemed to simply want to buy a gift his little friend would enjoy.

She wondered if he could possibly identify with the very tight budget she lived on while she tried to get her struggling business off the ground. Could someone who'd never had to count pennies understand what it was like to worry about paying next month's rent?

"Where do I pay for this?" he asked, hefting the sizable box.

"At the front register on your way out."

"Okay, thanks." He gave her another small smile. "You've been very accommodating."

She swallowed, forcefully holding her own smile in place. "I'm glad I could help. Is there anything else I can do for you?"

He seemed to have been waiting for that very question. He replied without hesitation. "Yes. You can have dinner with me some night soon."

It wasn't totally a surprise, but she still blinked a couple of times before frowning at him. "I thought we'd already covered this subject. It's nice of you to ask, but I'm going to have to decline."

"Because we're both too busy," he said, quoting her excuse from before.

She lifted her chin. "That's right."

It was even true—if not the whole truth.

"There's always time to eat a meal."

He didn't sound argumentative. Not even particularly determined to change her mind. He was simply stating a fact, she decided.

She answered in kind. "Well, yes, there's always time for a meal. But—"

"But not with me."

"It's nothing personal."

He cocked an eyebrow at her, making it clear he didn't buy that, either.

Sighing, she shook her head. "Okay, maybe it's a little personal. You make me nervous, James."

He looked startled, then chagrined. "I'm sorry. You needn't worry about me bothering you again, Shannon. I'm really not…I just thought…well, never mind. I'll just go pay for this now."

Grimacing, she caught his arm when he would have hurried away. "I didn't mean that the way it sounded."

But he'd gone stiff in response to her thoughtless comment and she couldn't begin to read his expression now. There was no evidence of his intriguing little half-smile when he drew away. "It's okay. I understand. Thanks again for your help."

"James—"

"Excuse me, miss, do you work here? I'm looking for that new Perky Pet that's so popular." The elderly customer glanced uncertainly from Shannon to James as if sensing she might have interrupted something more than a retail transaction.

James took advantage of the interruption to nod a goodbye to Shannon and disappear with his purchase.

Smoothing both her expression and the bright green vest that marked her as a store employee, Shannon focused on her new customer. "Yes, ma'am, we have a whole display devoted to Perky Pets. Follow me and I'll show you the newest selections."

She would mentally replay that clumsy interlude with James later, she predicted with an inner wince. She was quite sure she would come up with exactly the right things to have said, now that it was too late to correct her tactless blunder.

James had spent the entire month of August doing an AI, or Acting Internship, in pediatrics. It had been a demanding rotation, with only four days off during the month—one of which he'd spent at the lake where he'd met Shannon and her family. Still, he'd enjoyed the experience, finding it instructive and mentally challenging, both requirements he craved in his daily activities.

As the name implied, his duties mimicked those of a true medical intern, giving him experience for whatever residency program he would enter after his graduation in May. Beginning work at seven each morning, he carried the same patient load as an intern, wrote daily progress notes on the patients, made presentations during daily rounds and even wrote orders, though his orders had to be cosigned by a resident. He carried a pager and had been on call a couple of times, sleeping in the call room as did the regular pediatric residents.

The evaluations of his performance had been glowing, as far as his medical skills. He was noted as punctual, conscientious, perceptive and professional. He had excelled in the first two years of medical school, comprehending the lectures and acing the tests so that he'd entered the third year at the top of the class. No real surprise; he had entered medical school having already obtained a Ph.D in microbiology, so he'd had a solid foundation for the material in the lectures.

And yet, when it came to his communication skills, the remarks were less enthusiastic. And that frustrated him to no end.

His conversational abilities were fine. Having grown up in an academic household, he could express himself clearly, easily explain even the most complicated terms and hold his own in a debate. Spending time with his study-group friends the past three years had taught him more about making small talk and lightening tense moments with a smile and a quip— things he hadn't learned from his intensely serious parents.

While it had been made clear from the beginning that physicians had to maintain a professional distance, and while some specialties required less personal interaction than others, James was primarily interested in the pediatric infectious disease practice. With his strong academic and research background in microbiology, he believed he had much to offer to the field. Yet dealing with the emotions of patients and their worried parents was very much a part of that specialty and James wondered sometimes if he'd ever master that particular skill.

It wasn't that he didn't care about the ailing children. Obviously he did, or he wouldn't even consider dedicating the rest of his life to curing them. Nor was he hardened to the emotional toll a child's illness took on the rest of the family. He always felt as if he was saying the right things, behaving as the situation required—and yet he still kept getting those vaguely worded evaluations about how he needed to work on his communication skills.

He was growing increasingly frustrated with that situation. How was he to maintain a professional distance and still empathize with the patients? How did one learn to express the optimum mixture of competency and compassion? If only there were some formula to memorize or some protocol to learn, he'd have no problem, but this was an intuitive, indefinable quality he wasn't sure he possessed.

Obviously, he'd been less than successful in communicating with Shannon Gambill, he thought glumly, making a note in a patient chart before completing his duties on the last Thursday of his Acting Internship. He'd thought he'd been friendly and pleasant, just persistent enough to make his interest clear. Shannon had seen his behavior differently.

You make me nervous, James.

He still winced when he remembered those words. Apparently he'd come on too strong or too…something. It had certainly never been his intention to make her uncomfortable.

He supposed he really was lousy at this communication thing.

"Hey, James, how's it going?"

Looking up from the chart in response to the greeting, James smiled at the slightly rumpled, sandy-haired medical student approaching from the end of the hallway. "Hi, Ron. I'm doing well, how about you?"

His friend Ron Gibson was also completing an AI in pediatrics, though Ron was assigned to pediatric oncology and hematology, or pedi hem-onc in medical jargon. Twenty-eight-year-old Ron had become one of James's two closest male friends since they'd joined the same five-person study group in the first semester of their freshman year of medical school. Charming, laid-back and affable, Ron had struggled a bit during the first two years of classwork and exams, but he excelled in clinical practice, becoming an instant favorite with the very sick children he wanted to spend his career treating.

Ron seemed to have no problem at all communicating, James thought a bit glumly as he dropped the patient chart into the wall-mounted holder outside the hospital room. "What are you doing on this wing?"

"Looking for you. Haley, Connor and I are meeting for dinner this evening. Connor's at loose ends tonight because Mia and Alexis are doing something girly and he thought it would be a good time to catch up. Want to join us?"

James didn't even have to think about it. "Sure. What time?"

Moving to the next room on his assigned patients' list after Ron went back to his own duties, James drew a deep breath as he picked up the chart and flipped through it. He pasted on a smile before entering, trying to add a little of Ron's natural warmth to the expression.

It came so easily to Ron—why did James have to work so hard at it, when all he wanted to do was help his patients?

The Italian restaurant where the group had decided to meet was surprisingly busy for a Thursday evening. Looking for his friends, James entered past a crowd waiting for tables in the lobby. He wasn't in the greatest of moods after his tiring day. It didn't help that this restaurant was on the same street as the toy store where Shannon worked—as if he had needed that reminder.

Still, he looked forward to visiting for a little while with Connor and Ron and Haley. It was so rare for them to get together now that they were all on such different schedules. He'd miss seeing Anne, the only remaining member of the original study group, but since Ron hadn't mentioned her joining them, he assumed she'd had other obligations.

A slightly harried-looking hostess gave him a vague smile when he approached. "How many, sir?"

"Actually, I'm meeting some people here. I don't know if they're here yet... Oh, there they are." Never shy about calling attention to himself, Ron stood at a table across the busy dining room, waving his arms to get James's attention.

Even though it was still five minutes before the agreed-upon meeting time, James was the last to arrive. He took the chair next to Connor, across the table from Ron and Haley.

Thirty-four-year-old Connor Hayes was the senior member of the group, having taught and coached for a few years before entering med school. James remembered how tough that first semester had been for his friend. Only a couple of months into his training, Connor had become fully responsible for the then-six-year-old daughter whose existence had been a secret to him before that time. Had it not been for his friend Mia, now his wife of just over two years, who had stepped forward to help him with Alexis, Connor might well have had to drop out of medical school in his first year.

Which would have been a shame, James thought, because there was such a shortage of primary-care doctors, which was what Connor wanted to practice. Connor would be an excellent family practitioner.

James looked curiously around the full dining room. "I

don't think I've ever seen it so busy here. Especially on a weeknight."

Ron chuckled. "You don't even know it's half-price lasagna night, do you?"

"Is it?" James shrugged, now comprehending the restaurant's popularity. "I guess that explains it. Maybe I've just never been here on a Thursday before."

"Like you'd ever have to wait in line to save a few bucks on some pasta," Ron joked.

"I appreciate a bargain as much as the next guy," James assured him, taking no offense at the teasing. Ron joked with everyone. James had figured out long ago that it was never intended mean-spiritedly. Ron just liked laughing and encouraging people to laugh with him.

Like the others, James ordered the lasagna. He was well aware his friends were all on limited budgets as they completed medical school on student loans. He would've offered to pick up the check, but he'd tried that a couple of times early on and his friends had made it politely, but firmly, clear that they paid their own ways.

He'd always been very careful not to make an issue of his good fortune—after all, it wasn't as if he'd earned the money himself. He just happened to have been born into a wealthy family, which was nothing more than the luck of the draw as far as he was concerned. He had long since realized how true it was that money couldn't buy happiness. Or true friendship.

"Here's to tomorrow, the last day of the current rotation," Ron said, holding up his water glass. "One day closer to graduation."

Laughing, they joined in the toast with sips of water.

They chatted about their experiences during the past month's rotations, swapping amusing anecdotes and sharing tidbits they had learned. They were starting a new block the following week and that gave them something to discuss, as well. In addition, all of them would be spending time during the next few months doing away rotations in other states.

"I'm looking forward to my acting internship in Cincinnati in October," Haley said, then added candidly, "even if I'm a little nervous about it. I'm sure they'll do things differently than we do here."

"They'll love you there," Ron assured her, reaching over to squeeze her hand. "How could they not?"

She smiled back at him a little wistfully. "It will be a long month away from you."

"I'll be in Lexington. Not that far from Cincinnati," Ron replied with a shrug. "There's a chance we can get together at least one weekend during the month."

It would be the first time the newlyweds had been separated that long since they'd become engaged last December. Or maybe even before that, James mused, thinking of all the hours the study group had spent together during their first two years of school, before Haley and Ron had realized that the sparks they'd set off each other from the start had been due to more than temper.

James still shuddered to remember how close they'd come to losing Haley last December. He suspected Ron still had nightmares about the life-threatening injury Haley had sustained in a rare winter tornado that had brought down the ceiling of a diner where they had taken shelter, driving a piece of metal through Haley's leg. She'd been airlifted to the trauma unit but because of blood loss, her condition had been dicey during the trip. Yet, with typical Haley optimism and determination, she had been back in rotations five weeks later, missing only one rotation she had been able to reschedule for fourth year, so that she would graduate with the rest of them.

Their wedding had been a small affair at the end of June, giving them only a week for a honeymoon. Neither had wanted an elaborate wedding—partially because of time constraints, but also because of finances. Neither of them came from an affluent family and both were attending medical school on student loans. They had married beneath a gazebo in a local park. James thought the simple ceremony had been as touching as any elaborate wedding he'd ever reluctantly attended.

"October's going to be a tough month for Mia," Connor commented as he sliced into the steaming pasta that had just been set in front of him. "With me in Chicago, she'll be fully responsible for Alexis, in addition to her grad-school work and her teaching position."

Connor's guilt was evident to all of them. Typically, Haley was the first to offer encouragement. "They'll be fine while you're gone, Connor. Mia loves being with Alexis and vice versa. It isn't as if Alexis is any trouble. She's a good kid."

From what James had observed, completing medical school while maintaining personal relationships was a tricky balancing act. Med school required total commitment, leaving little free time for family and friends, especially during those first two years of endless classes and studying. Fourth year wasn't so bad, other than the highly recommended away rotations, but then would come residency programs. Everyone knew how many hours a medical resident spent at the hospitals.

James was aware of several marriages that had ended among his classmates during the past three years. But for his study-group friends, he was very optimistic that their romantic partnerships would endure.

Mia had been well prepared for what she was getting into when she'd married a single-father medical student. She had made it clear she considered the short-term sacrifices worth the effort to allow Connor to follow his dream, just as she was pursuing her own doctorate in education. Anne Easton had been through a rocky spell with her husband, Liam McCright, but that was due more to family issues than the demands of medical school. And Haley and Ron were certainly prepared to make the compromises necessary to be successful both in their careers and their relationship.

James had dated occasionally, but only casually. His record with relationships wasn't particularly encouraging even without the demands of his career training to further complicate matters. Surreptitiously studying the smiles Haley and Ron exchanged, he was aware of a slight pang of…something. It felt almost like wistfulness, though he brushed that thought aside quickly. Apparently he was letting himself be affected by the rosy romances of his friends. He was the only single member left of this group, to whom he had become so close during the past three years.

Pulling his gaze from the happy couple, he glanced away from the table—only to have his glance intercepted by a pair of familiar green eyes.

No way, he thought, swallowing a groan. What were the odds that Shannon would show up here at this moment? Of course, the restaurant was only a few blocks from where she worked. And it was half-price lasagna night. But still, of all the restaurants in Little Rock…

This would probably give her even more reason to believe he was stalking her, he thought glumly. Even though he'd obviously arrived first, since she was just being led to a table along with another woman. And even though he was there with friends of his own.

She hesitated momentarily and he wondered if she was deciding whether to nod acknowledgment or pretend she hadn't seen him. But then she stopped by his table and gave him a bright smile, motioning for her friend to continue on. "Hello, James."

He could do polite and casual as well as she. "Hi, Shannon. How are you?"

"Fine, thank you. You?"

He nodded. "Can't complain. Here for the lasagna?"

"Of course. Best in town."

"Enjoy your meal."

"Thanks. You, too." After another slight pause, she nodded affably to him and his companions, then turned and walked across the dining room to join her friend at a small booth on the other side. She slid into the booth with her back to the table where James sat, so the only part of her he could see was the top of her curly red hair.

He reached for his iced tea, trying to focus again on his friends. "Have you heard from Anne this week, Haley? How's she doing on her family-practice rotation?"

But Haley was looking from Shannon's booth to James and back again, while Ron and Connor stared curiously at James.

"What?" he said, frowning in response to their expressions.

"What was *that?*" Ron blurted, motioning vaguely in Shannon's direction.

James shifted a little in his seat. "Just someone I've met a couple of times. I hardly know her."

"Uh-huh." Ron made no secret of his skepticism.

On the defensive now, James set his glass back down without tasting the beverage. "What?" he said again. "Was I rude? Should I have introduced her to everyone?"

He probably should have, he chided himself. He should have introduced her to Connor, especially. He wasn't quite sure why he hadn't.

"I think Ron is referring to the tension between the two of you," Haley suggested, studying James's face with enough avid interest to make him squirm again. "Wow."

"I don't know what you're talking about." Seeking reinforcement, James glanced toward Connor.

Connor shrugged apologetically. "Sorry pal, I felt it, too. Could have cut the air between you with a scalpel."

"You should have called her after taking her out," Ron suggested, making a wild guess at the cause of that tension.

"I've never taken her out," James replied somewhat stiffly.

Ron widened his blue eyes dramatically. "She shot you down? Seriously? The woman is immune to James Stillman's notorious magnetism?"

James felt his cheeks warm a bit—irritation, he assured himself—even as Haley shook her head. "She wasn't immune. Trust me on that. Whatever else was going on, she was definitely not immune."

"So why did she turn him down when he asked her out?" Ron inquired, turning slightly on his chair to look at Haley.

"He must have made a mess of asking her."

Ron goggled dramatically. "James? Dr. Smooth? Dr. Every Ladies' Dream? Dr.—"

"Okay, Ron, that's enough," Haley interrupted drily, to James's relief. "I think you've made your point."

"I'd say so," James grumbled, stabbing his fork rather viciously into a noodle, even though he'd pretty much lost his appetite.

Always the encourager, the one Ron always flippantly referred to as the class cheerleader, Haley smiled across the table. "You should ask her out again, James. I mean, you're obviously attracted to her and she wouldn't have stopped to say hello if she wasn't interested in return."

"You know, she looked a little familiar," Ron commented before James had a chance to come up with a response to Haley's advice. "Have we met her before?"

"She looked familiar to me, too," Haley agreed.

James shrugged. "I just met her myself a couple weeks ago. Now, could we please discuss something else?"

The others looked at him oddly, as if they weren't accustomed to seeing him so disconcerted. He supposed they weren't. He usually maintained his composure in front of other people, having been drilled from childhood to keep his problems and negative emotions to himself. "No one's interested in attending your pity party," had been one of his father's favorite sayings.

Haley responded immediately to his strained request. "Of course. So, Connor, how is Alexis? I haven't seen her in a while, is she still growing by leaps and bounds?"

"She is," Connor replied. "We had to buy all new uniforms for the upcoming school year because she's outgrown all the ones from last year. Hard to believe she's going to be nine in a couple of weeks. Remember, anyone who's available that weekend is invited to drop by the day of the party for munchies and cake. We're going to keep the kids in the backyard and the adults can mingle in the den. Mia and I will be running back and forth, but the party organizer said she'll do most of the kid-wrangling."

Which wasn't exactly a change of topic, James thought with a wince, even though Haley and Connor had been trying to help him out.

James swallowed a gulp of wine, then blurted, "That woman who just spoke to me? Shannon? She's the one Mia hired to organize Alexis's birthday party."

Three sets of surprised eyes turned his way again. He'd had to tell them, he reminded himself. They'd find out for themselves soon enough.

"No kidding?" Connor glanced in the direction of the booth. "She's the one you suggested I recommend to Mia?"

"Yeah. You said Mia could use some help and I'd just met Shannon. I knew she was a kids' party planner, so I sent Mia the Web site address."

"Very interesting," Ron murmured, then winced. James

suspected Haley had kicked Ron beneath the table to keep him from starting up his teasing again.

"Well, she looked nice," Haley asserted. "I bet she's good at her job."

"I hope so," James murmured, feeling the responsibility of being the one to recommend Shannon for Alexis's party. "I saw her in action with her nieces and nephews, and she was really good at organizing them. They're obviously crazy about her."

Connor shrugged. "Mia checked out the Web site pretty closely. She wouldn't have hired Shannon if she didn't think it would work out. It's not like we wanted anything fancy or extravagant. Just a simple kids' party with a few decorations and a couple of craft projects to keep them entertained. Mia could have done it herself if she weren't so crazy busy right now."

He glanced at James. "It was my idea to invite some of our adult friends, too. Since Mia's birthday is just a few weeks away, and I'll be getting ready to leave for the away rotation then, it seemed like a good idea to sort of combine the two celebrations. It's going to be a real casual thing. Mia and I will keep an eye on the kid party and take some pictures, but Alexis is at the age where she doesn't want us hovering over her and her friends," he added with a rueful expression. "She liked the idea of us having our own friends to play with inside."

Ron chuckled. "Wait until she starts inviting boys to her parties. She's really going to want you to disappear then."

Connor scowled. "That's when I'm going to be even more visible. I'm just glad she wanted only girls at this party."

Delighted to have a new target to tease, Ron began to taunt Connor with predictions of Alexis as a pretty teenager, bring home her first boyfriend, going to dances and prom. Groaning and reluctantly laughing, Connor didn't have to entirely fake his dismay. He'd had his little girl for only three years, he said. He hated to think of her growing up that fast.

Though the group lingered for a short time over post-meal coffees, Connor was the one who eventually brought the evening to an end. "Mia and Alexis should be home now," he commented with a glance at his watch. "I'd like to spend a little time with them before Alexis's bedtime."

James wondered if Ron's hints about teenage years had made Connor want to hurry home to savor his daughter's childhood as much as possible.

"We should be getting home, too," Haley murmured, reaching for her bag. "Ron and I both have to report at seven in the morning."

Aware that he was the only one going home to an empty apartment, James was sorry to see the dinner with his friends end. For the first time in his life, he felt truly a part of a closely knit group, and he enjoyed every moment with them. Like Connor, he was keenly aware of passing time. After graduation in May, the study group would be going in different directions for their residency programs. It would be harder to get together in the future. He would miss them all very much.

He shook Ron's hand in the parking lot, then watched Ron and Haley walk away, Ron's arm slung casually around Haley's shoulders. James noted in satisfaction that Haley didn't even limp when she walked now, a sign that she was fully recovered from her injuries. Connor was already in his car when James walked to the far side of the lot, which was the only place he'd found to park when he'd arrived among the dinner rush.

Pushing the unlock button on his key-fob remote, he eyed the sensible little hybrid he'd recently purchased without a great deal of enthusiasm. Until recently, he had driven a vintage, classic sports car, which he had loved more than any inanimate object he'd ever owned. Something about that cherry-red convertible he'd named Terri, for no particular reason, had appealed to him from the first time he'd seen it. Maybe because he'd known his father would heartily disapprove?

Unfortunately, Terri was a temperamental and unreliable mistress, leaving him stranded at the most inconvenient times. Despite his first-name relationship with every decent mechanic in the area, James had finally conceded he needed more reliable transportation for his career. He'd put Terri in storage for someday when he had time to play with her again. In the meantime, he was driving a vehicle that his dad considered sensible and responsible, and privately wondering if he was destined to turn into his dad despite his small rebellions.

He was just reaching for the door handle when a woman's voice spoke from behind him. "James? Could we talk for a minute?"

He dropped his hand, then steeled himself to turn to face Shannon.

Chapter Four

Shannon wasn't known to be timid under any circumstances and rarely had difficulty speaking her mind. She freely admitted there were times when she was too quick to speak, blurting out whatever ran through her head, a tendency she had to fight on a daily basis. She'd always believed somewhat ruefully that she'd inherited the tendency from her mother's side of the family.

So, she didn't know why she was having so much trouble trying to decide what to say to James. Maybe because her runaway mouth had made such a hash of things when she'd spoken with him in the toy store. Not that she could tell by looking at him that she had ruffled him in the least. His expression was distantly courteous, and his shuttered dark eyes held no particular emotion. The faint smile that could be charming and intriguing was merely polite now.

"Yes?" he prompted when her hesitation lasted a bit too long.

"I'm not sure I thanked you properly for recommending my services to your friend. At this stage in my business, word-of-mouth referrals are very important."

"You thanked me at the toy store. But you're welcome. I know Alexis is looking forward to her party. That was her father sitting beside me at dinner, by the way. Sorry, I should have introduced you."

Though she wondered why he hadn't, she waved off the apology. "I'm sure I'll meet him at the party. The last time I spoke with her, Mrs. Hayes told me some of their friends and some of the children's parents are planning to watch a football game inside during the party. Will you be there?"

"I'm not sure yet. But don't worry, if I go, I'll stay well out of your way."

She sighed in response to his slightly stiff tone. "Okay, James? Let's just get this out of the way, shall we? I said something stupid in the toy store and you took it all wrong. When I said you make me nervous, it wasn't because I think you're a stalker or a weirdo or anything like that."

She had the satisfaction of seeing a genuine emotion on his face then—apparently she had caught him off guard with her blunt candor.

"Um—" Now it was James who seemed at a loss for words. Shannon had the impression that few people ever saw him flustered, as he seemed to be now.

He recovered quickly, his lips quirking into a hint of the smile she liked so much. "Thank you. I'm relieved to know you don't place me in either of those categories."

She really was a sucker for that formally courteous tone of his. Combined with his fleeting smiles—and those gorgeous eyes—it made it even more difficult for her to remember that she'd had good reason for being wary of the man.

It wasn't so much him she didn't trust, she admitted ruefully. It was herself around him.

"So what exactly is it about me that makes you nervous?" he asked, genuine curiosity evident in his voice.

This noisy parking lot was hardly the place for such a personal discussion, even though she was aware she was the one who had impulsively initiated it when she'd seen James standing by his car, parked not far from her own. Though the sun had not yet set, the shadows lengthened around them. The exhaust-scented air was warm and rather sticky against the skin exposed by the short-sleeve top she wore with summer-weight khaki pants. Patrons arriving and leaving talked and slammed car doors and a toddler cried noisily near the restaurant entranceway. Hardly an ideal place for the apology she was trying so awkwardly to make.

She had been so startled to see James dining here this evening. She and Devin had agreed to meet for half-price lasagna as Shannon was getting off work for the day and Devin was on her way to begin her shift. Shannon had nearly tripped over her own feet when she'd caught James's eyes on her way to her table. She could tell by the way he'd responded to her greeting that he was still stinging over the way they'd last parted.

She had realized then that rather than annoying him, her tactless words at the toy store had hurt his feelings. And that was a situation her conscience prodded her to rectify, even if she wasn't entirely sure how to go about it.

She drew a deep breath. "I just get the feeling you're one of those march-in-and-take-charge sort of guys and that's what makes me a little nervous. I mean, doctors are accustomed to giving orders and having them followed without question. Making decisions on behalf of other people. Telling people what's good for them. And I don't handle that sort of thing very well."

A jacked-up pickup truck passed on the busy road beside them, heavy bass blasting from the radio so loudly Shannon could almost feel her bones vibrate in response, drowning out the other sounds of cars and people milling in the restaurant parking lot. Instinctively, she threw an annoyed glare in the direction of the ugly truck, then turned back to James.

If he'd noticed the distraction at all, she couldn't tell by looking at him. His eyes were steady on her face, his expression thoughtful as if he were dissecting her words to study every nuance.

"You're very direct, aren't you?" he commented when he could be heard again over the fading boom box on wheels.

Making a face, she shrugged. "It's a family trait, I guess."

He nodded. Having spent a couple of hours with her outspoken and gregarious family, he probably understood her excuse very well.

She couldn't help thinking that James was pretty much her opposite when it came to outspokenness. Whereas she tended to blurt out whatever she was thinking, he kept his thoughts so well masked that there was no telling what was going on in that handsome head. Another potential point of conflict between them, she reminded herself. It would drive her crazy to be with someone who couldn't share what he was thinking or feeling.

"So, have you dated doctors before?" he asked, his tone uninflected. "Is that how you've derived your assessment of the physician's personality?"

She couldn't help but be wryly amused by the question. He was such an academic. "Sort of. I dated a—"

A blast of a car horn from the road drowned out her words. It was followed by a screech of tires that made her jump and look around, half expecting to see a wreck take place at the intersection. As it was, two cars barely avoided a collision, followed by curses shouted out an open window and a few hand gestures expressing displeasure with each others' driving.

"Holy—" She sighed, leaving the rest of her trademark phrase unspoken. "This really isn't the place for a discussion. Let's go to the coffee shop at the bookstore down the street where we can talk without shouting over the idiots on the road."

"Fine," he said without hesitation and opened his car door. "I'll meet you there."

Still muttering beneath her breath about crazy and inconsiderate drivers, Shannon climbed into the thirdhand, compact SUV she'd purchased for hauling around her party supplies and started the engine. She was halfway to the bookstore when it occurred to her abruptly what she had just done.

She'd asked James to join her for coffee. And he had accepted so smoothly it didn't even occur to her to have second thoughts. Amused and exasperated—with both of them—she laughed softly and promised herself that this would be as close to a date as she would get with James Stillman.

James motioned for Shannon to proceed him into the large, chain bookstore. The familiar scents of coffee and pastries greeted her when she entered this place where she spent quite a bit of time. She loved browsing through the books and magazines, sitting in the invitingly soft chairs scattered throughout the store and perusing pages of interesting-looking books to decide if she wanted to buy them, sipping overpriced coffee drinks and people-watching for a relaxing hour or two. Sometimes she brought her laptop and answered e-mail, worked on party plans or just surfed her favorite Web sites.

Maybe she'd look through the books after she and James had finished their friendly coffees, she thought. She hadn't bought a book in at least a week—she could probably squeeze another book purchase into this month's budget.

"Hey, James, how's it going?" the black-haired, heavily eye-lined, multiply-pierced young woman behind the coffee counter called out as they approached. "Got a new study partner?"

James chuckled. "I'm not studying tonight, Cass. Just having coffee with a friend."

"You want the usual?"

"Sure. What would you like, Shannon?"

She studied him with a raised eyebrow. As many hours as she'd spent in this store, she was rarely greeted by name and never offered "the usual" in the coffee shop. "Spend a little time here, do you?"

He smiled wryly. "I've spent hours in every coffee shop in central Arkansas. My study group always liked combining caffeine with cramming for tests."

Because it had been so warm and humid outside, leaving her feeling a little sticky, she opted for a cold drink. "Cinnamon dolce frappuccino," she requested, opening her purse.

James shook his head. "On me," he murmured, handing Cass his credit card. "I have a discount card here," he added as if that would ward off her automatic protest.

"So do I," she argued, anyway. "And I was the one who suggested this."

Cass swiped the card quickly, winking at James as she did so. "Too late. Already rang it up."

Sighing, Shannon let her shoulder strap purse drop back to her side. "Thank you."

There weren't a lot of customers in the coffee shop—or the bookstore, for that matter—on this Thursday evening. Two middle-aged women gossiped at one table, three teenage girls talked and texted at another, a college-age girl sat behind a stack of books in one corner, scribbling in a wire-bound notebook, and a law student clattered the keyboard of his computer on a little table filled almost to overflowing with law textbooks. Coffee shops and studying seemed to be a popular combination, Shannon mused as she and James claimed a little table in a deserted corner to wait for their drinks.

"So, you dated a…?" James prompted.

She blinked before realizing that he was taking up their conversation exactly where it had been interrupted before. She laughed.

"What?"

She shook her head. "You just amuse me."

"I thought you said I make you nervous."

"I've decided nervous is the wrong word," she admitted. "I'm not nervous around you, James."

"Good."

"The correct word would be wary. Definitely wary," she repeated, nodding in satisfaction with the choice.

His expression shifted from pleased to somber again. Maybe she was beginning to read him a little better, after all. It was quite obvious to her that he didn't like "wary" any better than he'd liked "nervous."

Cass set their drinks in front of them. "Let me know if you need anything else," she urged them before heading back to her station.

Shannon was usually called to the counter to pick up her own drink. No table deliveries for her.

James must be one generous tipper, she decided, taking a sip of the drink that even tasted slightly better than usual this evening. She nodded toward the steaming espresso James had ordered. "Isn't it a little late for that?"

He lifted one shoulder in a hint of a shrug. "I've developed a caffeine immunity in the past couple of years. Whenever I get a chance to sleep, I'm gone the minute I hit the pillow, even if I've had a whole pot of coffee beforehand."

"I've heard med school is a nightmare."

"The first two years are the most difficult. Third year involves long hours and a lot of procedures and information to learn. This year is a cakewalk in comparison, though it has its own challenges."

"You're at the top of the class, aren't you?"

He shifted a little uncomfortably in his chair in response to her deliberately blunt question. "I've done well enough."

"The top."

He shrugged. "I had the advantage of earning a Ph.D in microbiology before I entered med school, so the basic science was already familiar material to me."

She blinked. "You earned a doctorate before you started medical school?"

"Yes."

"How old were you when you graduated high school?"

He toyed with his coffee cup. "Sixteen. Both being educators, my parents thought it best for me to skip ahead of some of the early grades."

"So you'll be a double-doctor." She tried not to let him see that this new bit of information made him even more intimidating.

"I'll have an M.D.-Ph.D," he corrected, then changed the subject quickly away from his accomplishments. "You said you dated a doctor?"

He was determined to finish the conversation they had started in the parking lot. She supposed they might as well. Once he understood her qualms, he would realize it wasn't anything personal against him, she figured, and her conscience would be clear about hurting his feelings.

"I dated a dentist. He made a huge point of calling himself 'Doctor.' Introduced himself to everyone as Dr. Smith. Corrected people when they called him Mr. Smith," she added wryly. "He even signed a birthday card to me 'Dr. Philip Smith.'"

James looked uncomfortable again. "I know a few people like that," he murmured. "Somewhat pompous?"

"The very definition of pompous," she emphasized.

"So why did you get involved with him?"

"Because he was also charming and amusing and my family pressured me into ignoring my instincts and giving him a chance. And to be honest, I was on the rebound from another long-term relationship that had ended badly. Philip's attention was flattering—just what my bruised ego thought I needed at the time, I guess—and for a while, I let myself ignore the warning signs. He was always trying to make decisions for me, subtly criticizing my choices, assuring me he had my best interests at heart when he told me what I should or shouldn't do with my life."

She took another sip of her iced drink. "It finally occurred to me after dating him for several months that he was deliberately grooming me to be the companion he considered fitting for his status. I realized then that I was going to have to break up with him or break his pompous nose. I decided on the former—though the latter would have been much more satisfying," she added reflectively. "We broke up a little over a year ago, and since then I've focused on establishing my own identity."

"Was your former boyfriend—the one before Dr. Philip Smith—also a doctor? Or a dentist?"

"No. Greg was my high-school boyfriend. Captain of the football team, class vice president, leader of the popular crowd—you know the type. We were engaged for a couple of years after graduation while he went to a small, state college on a football scholarship after it turned out he wasn't quite good enough to play for any of the big schools. I took a few classes but never decided on a major, and then I tried a couple of unsuccessful jobs in search of an identity other than Greg's girlfriend and personal cheerleader. He dumped me for someone else when I stopped letting my life revolve entirely around him."

She lifted her glass to her lips again, more to shut herself up than because she particularly wanted another sip. She always tended to babble, she admitted freely—a Gambill family flaw—but something about James made her blab even more than usual. Maybe it was because he revealed so little of himself either in words or expressions, and she seemed to need to fill the silences between them with her own revelations.

Besides, she told herself with an attempt at rationalization, he *had* asked why she was so leery of take-charge men. She was merely answering him honestly.

"So, ignoring your earlier relationship, on the basis of one bad experience with a pompous dentist, you've sworn off all doctors as potential friends?"

Now she was the one to shift in her seat. He made it sound so petty when he phrased it that way. "That's not exactly what I said."

"What you said, exactly, is 'doctors are accustomed to giving orders and having them followed without question. Making decisions on behalf of other people. Telling people what's good for them.' Apparently, you're basing all that conjecture on your brief relationship with Dr. Smith."

She blinked a couple of times before saying, "Eidetic memory?"

"Just good recall. But you still haven't responded to what I asked."

The man was as tenacious as a pit bull. Totally focused on solving the puzzle of why she'd concluded she wouldn't date doctors. "You really are a scientist, aren't you?"

He frowned. "I'm just trying to understand."

"I'm not really accustomed to discussing my dating history with virtual strangers."

As he eyed her over the rim of his cup she felt her cheeks warm.

"You started this conversation. You approached me in the

parking lot of the restaurant and then invited me to join you here for coffee so we could discuss your reasons for turning down my dinner invitation," he said.

"Oh. I guess you're right. Sorry."

His gaze lingered on her wry smile in a way that had her reaching hastily for her iced drink. She suddenly felt a little too warm.

But his voice was bland when he said, "You don't have to apologize. Though I am curious as to why you felt the need to explain your reasoning for turning down my invitation. All you had to say was no. I realize I asked twice, but I got the message the second time. I wouldn't have asked again."

"I know. It's just—well, I hurt your feelings in the toy store, when I said you made me nervous. I really hate hurting people. I just wanted you to know it wasn't anything about you personally, just my own hang-ups."

"You thought you hurt my feelings."

"I know I did."

"Interesting."

She tilted her head. "What's that supposed to mean?"

Picking up his cup again, he murmured, "You're very intuitive. Most people don't—"

He drowned the rest of the sentence in another sip of espresso.

She had a feeling she knew what he'd started to say. Most people probably had a hard time reading his feelings, hurt or otherwise. He did seem to keep them well hidden. Was that a deliberate choice or just the way he was? Either way, it was another difference between them. Everyone always claimed her face revealed her every thought. Well, those thoughts she hadn't already expressed verbally, she added with a mental wince.

"So you think I'm pompous," he said, lowering his cup. "But you don't want to hurt my feelings about it because it's simply your personal hang-up that you don't date pompous men."

Startled, she shook her head. "I didn't say you were pompous. I've never seen you behave that way at all."

"Just a bossy, take-charge doctor-to-be, is that it?"

She struggled against a smile in response to his politely interested tone. "Well, you did pay for my coffee, even though I said you shouldn't. It starts with those little things."

He nodded. "Forgive me. Next time, the coffee's on you."

Her smile broke through. "It's a deal."

"So? When is the next time?"

Oh, wait. What had she just agreed to? "Um—"

"You have to say yes. You owe me a cup of coffee," he reminded her.

The totally unexpected glint of mischief in his dark eyes was nearly her undoing. If he was so totally wrong for her, would she really find him this appealing?

"I'd drive you crazy," she warned.

"Maybe," he admitted. "But, unlike you, I don't make up my mind before giving something a chance."

Her eyebrows rose. "Ouch."

He looked a bit surprised that the words had escaped him, even though he'd obviously been teasing a little. "Sorry."

"Don't apologize. I like it that you have a bit of a snippy side. I was beginning to wonder if you're just too perfect to be real."

Now he was frowning again. "Um—"

Rather pleased with herself, she reached for her purse. "I'm going to browse through the books for a while. Thanks for the coffee, James. I'll be seeing you."

"When?"

Smiling over her shoulder, she replied, "I'll let you know. Good night."

She was aware that he watched her as she left the coffee

shop and disappeared into the book racks. She added a little extra sway to her walk just for good measure.

All in all, she decided, that encounter had gone pretty well.

Nine days after his impromptu coffee date with Shannon, James was still trying to determine what, exactly, had been decided between them. He thought she'd agreed to see him again—if only for a cup of coffee—but she'd left so abruptly, without anything being planned for certain, that he still wasn't sure she intended to follow through. He hadn't heard from her since, but that hadn't kept her from popping into his head surprisingly often, considering he'd met her only three weeks before and had seen her only twice since.

He debated attending the Hayes party because he certainly didn't want to cause any awkwardness there. He decided to go for several reasons, primarily because he didn't want to miss one of the remaining opportunities to spend time with his friends. And he couldn't deny that he wanted to see Shannon again, even though they probably wouldn't have much chance to talk in private.

He couldn't say, exactly, why he was so intrigued by Shannon. With her red curls and dimpled, lightly-freckled face, she was cute—enchantingly cute—but not the Hollywood model of striking beauty. But then he tended to think some of those too-perfect faces looked rather cold and boring.

Her artless, outspoken manner of speaking often took him aback. He never knew exactly what she was going to say next or sometimes how to interpret what she'd already said. But he'd always been intrigued by a puzzle.

Her background couldn't be any more different from his own. Her freewheeling, noisy, demonstrative family would probably find his parents stodgy and reserved and intellectually elitist—which, of course, they were. He loved his parents, as much as they would let him, but he was fascinated by Shannon's family.

She hadn't exactly encouraged him to pursue her—just the opposite, in fact. Which was also a rather refreshing chance, he admitted ruefully. Without undue conceit, he was aware he was considered a "great catch." He had decent looks, money and a future in a profession many considered to be socially advantageous. The past few women he'd dated hadn't done a very good job of hiding their interest in all of those things, though he wasn't sure any of them had been particularly interested in the man behind those assets.

Shannon seemed to be wary of the very traits that drew others to him. A march-in, take-charge kind of guy, he paraphrased her assessment of him. He'd never seen himself in that light and he thought she exaggerated, for the most part. But he could concede he probably came across that way sometimes. He had been trained to exude confidence and competence, both of which came naturally to him in a way that expressing doubt and vulnerability did not.

Perhaps she was right to be skeptical. Perhaps the differences between them were too great even to consider pursuing more than a casual friendship. He had to admit, the convoluted romantic history she had so candidly revealed to him in the coffee shop had taken him aback. But then again, all he'd done at this point was ask her to dinner. Whether a shared meal would lead to anything more was anyone's guess.

He was greeted at the door of the Hayes house by Anne Easton, who was filling in on hosting duty while Mia and Connor checked in on the kids' party that had started half an hour earlier. Pretty, petite blonde Anne smiled when James brushed a kiss across her cheek in greeting. "It's good to see you, Anne."

"It's good to see you, too." Her tone was just a little wistful. "I miss getting together as often as we used to."

"Is Liam here?"

She beamed. "He is. Come in and say hi. He's heading out again next week."

The football game was already playing on the TV in the den, and the adults assembled there kept an eye on the action as they sat and talked or milled around the table where an assortment of snacks and beverages were temptingly arranged. A birthday cake for Mia sat in the place of honor in the center of the table, uncut as of yet.

Setting his gift for Alexis and a smaller present for Mia on a side table with a few other wrapped packages, James greeted Liam, Anne's globe-trotting adventurer husband, then exchanged hellos with Ron and Haley. They all encouraged him to fill a plate and join them to view the game. He didn't share their enthusiasm for the sport, but he would enjoy watching with his friends, anyway. A few other friends of Mia and Connor's were there. James acknowledged the ones he'd met in the past and introduced himself to the ones he hadn't, working the room with the ease of a lifetime of experience with social situations.

He heard faint strains of music and children's voices coming from beyond the kitchen door that led out to the backyard. For Alexis's sake, he was glad the weather had cooperated with the outdoor party plans. It was a beautiful early September day, warm but not stiflingly so, a few small clouds drifting like puffy white birthday balloons across the rich blue sky.

Shannon was out there with that party. He hoped it was going well, for her sake and for Alexis. Maybe he could just peek out in a few minutes and see for himself.

Mia and Connor entered the room at that moment. Mia carried a small digital camera and both were smiling. Judging from their expressions, James decided the kids' party was going well. He was the only one who had arrived while they were outside, so they greeted him with pleasure.

"Alexis gave us the sign that she wanted us to stop taking pictures and come inside to play with our own friends," Connor said with a laugh. "Shannon has the ten girls busy with handcrafts. They're having a great time."

"Thank you for recommending her, James," Mia added. "She's delightful. The kids love her. I think she could handle three times as many as we have out there without any problems."

"She's very organized," Connor agreed. "She and an assistant arrived this morning with decorations, folding tables, chairs and all the supplies needed for the activities. She supplied everything but the cake, and she would have arranged that, too, if we'd asked."

"I wanted to make and decorate the cake," Mia admitted with a self-conscious smile. "It made me feel like I was putting at least some effort into the party, even though I didn't have time to do anything else."

"It's a beautiful cake," Anne assured Mia. "I saw it when I arrived. You did such a nice job piping the purple accents onto the pink frosting."

Anne glanced at James then. "One of those small-world things—Shannon's assistant is a CNA at the hospital. Her name's Devin Caswell. I saw her leaving just as I arrived and we recognized each other because I just rotated through the post-op wing. Do you know her?"

James shook his head. Shannon hadn't mentioned even having an assistant, much less that she worked in his field. "No, as far as I know, I haven't met her. But I haven't spent much time in post-op."

"I think I'll hire Shannon for McKenzie's party, too," one of Mia's friends said, overhearing the conversation. "McKenzie wants a karaoke party, of all things. A rock-star-diva theme. I bet Shannon could arrange that."

"I'm sure she could," Mia replied. "The girls would love that."

"My nephew has a birthday coming up in a couple of months," Anne mused aloud. "I'll mention Shannon's services to my sister-in-law next time I see her."

James was pleased that Shannon was doing so well today. He'd like to think he'd helped her establish her business a bit more. Of course, had she not done a good job for Mia, there would be no enthusiastic endorsements to encourage the others.

He was even more tempted now to steal a peek at her at work.

Shannon loved the chattering and giggling of the little girls surrounding her in the Hayes's tidy backyard. Kids having fun—that was the purpose of the business she'd put so much of her heart and soul into during the past months.

Devin had followed her here earlier to help set up before leaving to take care of other responsibilities that day. Together, they had decorated the area with pink and purple helium-filled balloons tied to every available anchor, and with a birthday banner Shannon had painted and hand-lettered stretched between two trees that shaded the Hayes family's picnic table. Though simple, the bobbing balloons and glittering sign, along with cheery paper lanterns in the tree branches, provided a festive backdrop for the event. And the birthday girl's parents hadn't had to do a thing to help, leaving them free to prepare for their other guests inside.

A pink-and-purple birthday cake decorated by Alexis's mom sat in the center of the picnic table, next to a bowl of frothy pink, fruit-flavored punch Shannon had brought with her. She had provided purple plastic dessert dishes and stemmed plastic goblets, arranged two big bouquets of inexpensive but colorful mixed flowers and scattered pink and purple faux gems across the frilly pink tablecloth. The table looked lovely, if she did say so herself, and the girls seemed suitably impressed. Shannon had even dressed to coordinate with the theme, wearing a rich purple top with nice jeans and purple ballet-style flats—casual and comfortable enough for her active role, but still flattering and stylish.

Alexis was a sweetheart. Bubbly and gregarious, she was generous with her guests, happily sharing the attention and the goodies. Shannon always began her parties with the gift-opening part. She liked the guests to leave with memories of fun and camaraderie rather than any natural jealousies over the birthday child's presents.

Once the gifts were opened, it was time for the activities. Ten little girls, while noisy and excitable, cooperated eagerly with Shannon's agenda. She had brought two folding crafts tables and ten small folding chairs. The girls squealed in anticipation when Shannon opened several boxes of crafts supplies they could use to decorate the ten unbleached muslin tote bags she'd brought along. She'd provided a colorful assortment of fabric markers, gingham bows, silk flowers, big buttons and glittering plastic "gems" to be attached with a rapid-drying fabric glue. The gems matched the princessy theme of the party, not too young for nine-year-olds, but just glam enough to spark their imaginations.

With a glittering, faux-jewel-enhanced birthday tiara perched on her light brown hair, Alexis flitted around the crafts tables, admiring everyone else's handiwork so much that she sometimes neglected her own. Twice Shannon guided her gently back to her chair, promising she would assist anyone who needed help while Alexis finished her own project.

Shannon supervised their work closely, but subtly, making sure the crafters weren't so liberal in their application of the adhesive that it would take too long to dry. The glue would set while the girls ate birthday cake and played a few games afterward. She'd brought lots of fun, inexpensive trinkets for game prizes, and she would make sure everyone left with something in addition to the party favors Mrs. Hayes had requested.

Of all the jobs Shannon had sampled during the past ten years or so, since she was old enough to drive herself to fill out employment applications, this business was the one she enjoyed the most. She'd worked in childcare and banking, had considered teaching and designing, even tried her hand at landscaping—but this, she thought, was the best thing she'd found thus far.

For the first time in her life, she felt like an independent adult. Living on her own income, renting a house with her equally independent friend, not accountable to her parents or a bossy boyfriend for how she spent her time or money. And she was running her own business, doing something she enjoyed and was good at.

Too bad she couldn't actually make a living at it. At least, not yet, she thought optimistically.

Standing to one side of the crafts tables, she laughed when one of the girls, Camryn, bragged over a particularly well-placed flower, which the other girls immediately copied on their own bags. There was a brief, tense moment when Camryn pouted over being copied, but Shannon quickly stepped in to congratulate her on providing such clever inspiration. Camryn decided to be flattered.

Shannon glanced at her watch. "Okay, everyone, five more minutes. We'll let the bags dry while we have cake and ice cream and then play a few games."

There was a quick scramble for more decorations to glue onto the bags. Shannon laughed again at their enthusiasm, then felt her smile fade when a funny tingling slipped down her spine. Swallowing, she turned slowly to glance toward the house.

James stood in the open doorway that led into the kitchen, watching her.

Slowly cleaning her glue-sticky hands on one of the dampened paper wipes available for that purpose, she was pleased he'd happened to look out just as all the girls were bent industriously over their crafts, obviously having a good time. For only a moment, she wished he could see her at one of her more elaborate parties—the medieval knights and princesses party she'd organized just last month, for example. Now that had been a blowout, few expenses spared by the doting parents for their rather spoiled daughter. She had several parties booked in the next few months as a result of that one, her most successful endeavor thus far.

This was a very simple little party, as Mrs. Hayes had requested, but it was a clear success. She supposed that was what counted, if…er, anyone should happen to be observing, judging her competence.

Seeing she had noticed him, James nodded. Even from where she stood, she could see his lips tilting into that sexy little smile. Her pulse rate tripped in response.

"Miss Shannon, will you help me decide where to put this bow?" one of the little girls asked.

Drawing her attention from James with an effort, Shannon turned back to her job, telling herself she would deal with James later.

Chapter Five

Parents arrived to collect their daughters right on time and it didn't take long to wrap up the kids' party. As she began to gather her decorations and supplies, Shannon judged the event an unequivocal success. The girls all seemed to be smiling as they departed, carrying party favors in their lavishly decorated tote bags.

"Let me help you haul some of that stuff to your car," Connor offered, handing the camera he'd been snapping to Mia, who was helping Alexis take her gifts inside.

"I'll help, too." Appearing suddenly at Shannon's side, James relieved her of the lidded plastic container she'd been holding.

"You guys don't have to do this," she protested, even as the men were already moving toward the front of the house with their loads. "Go back and join your friends. It will only take me a few minutes to—"

But they had already rounded the corner of the house,

leaving her talking to thin air. Sighing, she began to pack away the last of the supplies she'd brought with her. She'd already gathered the trash. Alexis had begged her to leave the balloons and banner in place for now, to which her parents had indulgently agreed.

With Connor and James helping, it took only a few minutes to pack everything into her little SUV, which was filled almost to capacity. Connor closed the back liftgate cautiously, making sure nothing jutted out to prevent it from latching. "Just barely held it all," he said with a laugh.

Shannon smiled. "Thank you both for your help."

"You're welcome." Connor motioned toward the house. "Would you like to come in for coffee? We've got the game on inside. The last quarter's just starting."

Remembering James's admission that he wasn't at all interested in football, not even the team most Arkansans cheered for, she glanced his direction. "Go, Hogs," he murmured, as he had before.

Sharing that memory, they smiled at each other.

"We would all love to have you join us for coffee," Connor said, glancing from Shannon to James and back again.

She twisted her car keys in her hands. "Thank you, but I'd better be on my way. I still have to get all this stuff unpacked and put away."

Connor nodded, then shook her hand and thanked her again for her services. "It was a nice party. Alexis had a great time. You really saved a lot of work for Mia and me."

"I enjoyed meeting you all. Alexis is adorable. She and her friends were one of the best-behaved groups I've worked with."

Connor grimaced humorously. "Yes, well, they have their moments."

He glanced at James again, then took a step backward.

"I'd better get back inside. Thanks again for everything, Shannon."

James lingered when Connor moved away. "Sounds like your party was a hit."

"I think so. It was hardly elaborate, but the girls seemed to have fun."

James lifted a shoulder in a light shrug. "Doesn't have to be elaborate to be a success. Mia said she would never have been able to put together all the craft supplies and the games and prizes and decorations you provided on such short notice, especially with her schedule. She and Connor are both receiving their advanced degrees in May, so maybe things won't be quite so hectic for them after that, though with him in residency and her looking for an administrative position in education, they'll always be busy."

She grinned. "Busy parents mean good business for me."

"Sounds like you'll be getting some calls from Mia and Connor's friends. They're impressed with what they've seen today. Everyone could see that you're very good at what you do."

Pleasure flooded through her. There was no compliment he could give her that would delight her more. She'd spent her entire life as the indulged baby sister or the supportive girlfriend. It felt good to be seen a competent and successful businesswoman. Success, she reminded herself, was not always synonymous with money.

"You're sure you don't want to come in for coffee?"

"No, I really can't. But I haven't forgotten that I owe you a cup."

He looked at her questioningly and she couldn't blame him for not being quite sure how to interpret her comment. After all, it had been over a week since she'd assured him coffee was her treat the next time. She had wondered if she would still be as attracted to him upon seeing him again after that interval. She'd had her answer the moment she'd looked up to see him watching her from the kitchen doorway and her knees had almost liquefied in reaction. His matter-of-fact praise of her career skills had only made him more appealing to her.

Maybe her instincts had overreacted a bit where James was concerned. Maybe her initial summary of him as a march-in, take-charge kind of guy wasn't exactly correct. He'd certainly given her little reason to believe that thus far. Maybe she had mistaken composure and self-assurance for an authoritarianism he did not possess. As he had pointed out to her, she'd made up her mind about him without giving him a chance to correct what could be an erroneous first impression.

And even if it turned out she'd been right the first time, she'd learned how to deal with men like that, right? She knew now how to stand up for herself, how to protect herself from disappointment and heartbreak. So it was foolish of her to deny herself a chance to enjoy his company just for fear of where it might lead.

"Hang on." She dug into her purse and drew out one of the pink-and-black Kid Capers business cards she had designed and printed herself. "That's my cell number," she said. "If I don't answer, I'm probably working with a customer at the toy store, so just leave me a message and I'll call you back."

"And why will I be calling you?"

She rather liked the somewhat confused look on his face. Keeping him slightly off-balance was another way for her to stay in control. "You'll be calling to arrange a time when we can get together for that coffee."

His mouth quirking into a smile, he tucked the card into his pocket. "I'll look forward to it."

She climbed into her car and drove away without further conversation.

* * *

Though the days were still hot during the first week of September, evenings brought some relief. The air was still very warm, but tolerable, as Shannon and James strolled down President Clinton Avenue in Little Rock's River Market District on the Friday following the birthday party. After a couple of stormy days, the weather this evening was perfect, clear and fanned by a light breeze. Quite a few people mingled around them on the sidewalk.

It was the second Friday of the month, when many of the galleries and shops stayed open later for "2nd Friday Art Night," some even serving wine and appetizers to draw in potential customers. Shannon tried to keep most second Friday nights open to enjoy the atmosphere and see what was new each month.

Music drifted from several of the bars and restaurants surrounding them. It wasn't yet dark, but lights were already beginning to reflect across the surface of the fast-moving Arkansas River flowing adjacent to the Avenue. Between the buildings they passed, Shannon caught glimpses of the river and the thirty-three-acre Riverside Park. The park stretched eleven blocks and included playgrounds, a promenade lined with ten large sculptures and a blue-canopied, ten-thousand-seat riverside amphitheater in which a local band was performing to a smallish, but noisily enthusiastic audience. She'd attended several concerts there herself.

Yellow-and-red electric trolleys passed on the busy street. They carried tourists and locals alike to the hotels, bars, restaurants, shops and galleries, and on down the street to the Museum of Discovery, the Main Library, located in a renovated riverside warehouse, the Arkansas Studies Institute, with its impressive art gallery, and the Clinton Presidential Library at the end of the Avenue. Shannon's nieces and nephews loved riding the trolley. She'd accompanied them several times on daytrips to the bustling farmer's market and to the museums.

On the other side of the river sat the city of North Little Rock. Located along the north bank of the river were the busy minor-league baseball park, the almost-always-booked Verizon Arena, and the open-for-tours World War II submarine, the U.S.S. Razorback, which was the main draw of the Maritime Museum. She'd visited all of those attractions at some point, usually in the presence of various family members. High-rise buildings housing businesses and condos stabbed into the early-evening sky on both sides of the river.

Shannon loved the lakes, woods and hills of rural Arkansas, but she had to admit a weakness for this lively, bustling downtown area, as well. For a compulsive people-watcher like her, this was an ideal place to spend a leisurely Friday evening.

"This was a good idea," James commented when they paused to admire the art displayed in a gallery window. "I haven't spent much time in the River Market District since Ron moved out of his downtown condo and moved into Haley's apartment last spring."

She glanced at one of the old buildings ahead that had been converted into loft condominiums. "I was tempted to buy one of those cool lofts, but I decided to rent a house with my friend Devin, instead. We needed the extra storage room for party supplies and we can use the living room for meeting with clients."

"So Devin is your business partner?"

"No. The business is mine. Devin's a friend from school—well, she was in classes with my sister, Stacy, a couple of years ahead of me. She was looking for a roommate at about the time I decided to look for a house to rent, so Stacy suggested we move in together and it's worked out very well. She helps me out with my party business in exchange for me paying a few dollars more on the rent. It works out for both of us."

"Good for you."

"I got two more bookings as a result of the Hayes party last weekend. Thanks again for the referral."

"You've thanked me enough times for that. I really didn't do that much." He motioned around them at the many inviting doorways. "Is there anywhere in particular you'd like to go? Are you hungry?"

They'd agreed to meet in the parking lot behind the River Market Pavilion at six, giving them a couple of hours to explore the shops and galleries. "Not yet. Let's go in here. I love this store."

He followed her obligingly into a fair-market shop that sold items crafted by third world artisans. It was one of her favorite places to shop for gifts. Reasonably priced, unique merchandise, and she knew her money was put to good use. With James close behind her, she wandered through the shop, admiring the home-decor items, bags, jewelry and toys. Exotic music played from hidden speakers, promoting the CDs from around the world on sale near the cash register.

"You're very tactile, aren't you?" James commented, indicating that he'd been paying more attention to her than the merchandise.

Letting a handwoven scarf trail through her fingers, she smiled. "I am. I have to touch everything displayed in stores, especially anything that looks soft or silky or textured. It drives my sister crazy because it takes me twice as long as her to shop."

He reached around her to pluck the colorful fringed scarf from the display peg, wrapping it around her shoulders like a jaunty shawl. "Looks good on you."

She laughed softly and savored the feel of the fabric around her shoulders. In deference to the late-summer heat, she'd worn a sleeveless green cotton top with a flowing, midthigh-length patterned skirt and woven green flats. The green, red, yellow and purple striped scarf added a brightly bohemian touch to her outfit, and felt good against the artificially chilled air brushing her skin from an overhead vent.

"It's beautiful, isn't it? I love picturing it on a loom in—" She checked the tag. "In Ecuador, with a skilled weaver choosing just the right threads and pattern."

James flicked the tag on a deep purple silk scarf. "This one's from India."

She pointed to others displayed on the same wall. "That one's from Bolivia. And here's one from Nepal. And another from Bangladesh. That's why I love to shop here, knowing those talented artisans all around the world are being paid fairly for their beautiful work."

Standing close in front of her, he made a slight adjustment to the scarf she still wore. "You have a big heart. And a big imagination."

His proximity—not to mention his touch—made her mouth go a bit dry. She moistened her lips and tried to speak casually. "I have to use my imagination. I'm an armchair traveler, I'm afraid. I've never left the continental U.S. and I haven't traveled that much within those borders. What about you? Have you been to any of the places where these scarves were made?"

"Yes." Without elaboration, he turned to pick up a paperweight made of a river rock decorated with a swirling pattern of brilliantly red goldfish. "This is nice."

"I have one of those on the writing desk in my bedroom. They're from Vietnam. The scales on the fish are made with the thumbprints of the artist. Each one is unique."

He looked at her again, his dark eyes gleaming like the lacquered stone in his hand. She swallowed, wondering if her artless mention of her bedroom had sparked the sudden flare of tension between them. Or was she the only one now picturing James in that particular room of her house? His expression was so hard to read; maybe she was simply projecting her own unbidden fantasies.

Dragging her gaze from his, she reached up to remove the scarf, which was priced a little higher than she could afford to spend just then. "Why don't we walk down to the Arkansas Studies Institute art gallery next? I've haven't seen the new exhibits there yet, have you?"

"No." He caught her hand before she could take off the scarf. "I don't suppose you'd let me buy that for you? It looks good on you."

She twisted a little, stepping out of his reach as she slid the scarf from her shoulders and returned it to its peg. "Thank you, but no. It's still a little too warm for it, anyway."

He looked at the scarf with a frown and for a moment she worried that he was going to try to overrule her and buy the scarf anyway, the way he had with the coffee at the bookstore. To her relief, he merely nodded and turned away, carrying the paperweight to the register to purchase for himself.

They spent some time in the four galleries of the Arkansas Studies Institute perusing the paintings, drawings, sculptures and other art, mostly by artists with Arkansas connections. She realized immediately that James had a keen interest in art, and a good eye for unique talent. It was a pleasure to walk beside him and listen to his analyses of the various pieces, and she encouraged him to continue when he hesitated as if in concern that he was boring her.

She couldn't imagine being bored by James. Perplexed, maybe. Discomfited. Intrigued and aroused. She could even imagine having her heart broken by him. But she doubted she would ever find him boring.

They were walking toward the exit when James paused to examine a small watercolor in the retail gallery. Depicting a rose garden with a copper watering can lying on its side in the dirt, the little painting wasn't up to the standards of some of the ones they had admired, but something about it seemed to catch James's attention. Studying his face, she made an effort to decipher his expression. His features were as smoothly composed as always, but there was something about the set of his mouth…

He turned her way, smiling a little when he saw that she was looking at him. "Ready to go? I don't know about you, but I'm a little hungry."

Glancing at the watercolor again, she decided to wait before asking him about it, to give herself time to mull over whatever she had seen in his face. "I could eat."

Accompanying her out the door and back onto the sidewalk, he named several restaurants within walking distance. Several of them were out of Shannon's usual price range and certainly didn't fit into this month's budget. She usually ate in the Market Hall food court, where a wide assortment of international dishes were available for very reasonable prices. But the food court was already closed for the evening, so she motioned to an establishment only a block away. "How about burritos?"

She'd eaten there before and knew she could afford the prices. Besides, she liked burritos.

Again, his expression showed no particular reaction. He merely nodded and fell into step beside her toward the invitingly open front of the burrito establishment. The front wall was made up of lifting glass doors; in nice weather like this, the only barrier between the tables and the sidewalks was a low wrought iron fence, giving an illusion of dining outdoors.

As the shops and galleries closed for the evening, more people milled on the sidewalks. The bars and clubs were just getting wound up for the Friday-night crowd. Shannon could hear strains of several types of music coming from open doorways.

"This is on me," she told James firmly as they stood in line to order. She already had her credit card in her hand and the look she gave him dared him to argue with her.

He tried, anyway. "Dinner is more than the cup of coffee you said you owed me."

"Don't care. It's still my treat."

He swept her face with an assessing look, then shrugged. "Thank you."

His unexpectedly quick capitulation made her smile in satisfaction. "Order whatever you want," she told him magnanimously.

His gaze locked on her mouth, long enough to make her smile quiver before he lifted his eyes slowly to hers. "I'll do that," he murmured.

Resisting an urge to fan her face with her hand, she glanced quickly at the menu board, trying to concentrate on burrito fillings rather than the enigmatic and so darned fascinating man at her side.

They were lucky to find a little table right on the railing, an ideal spot for watching the parade of people on the sidewalks. James had ordered fish tacos and a beer, subtly choosing one of the less expensive options on the reasonably priced menu. Shannon had a chicken burrito and a diet cola. Between the delicious, but messy food and the noise and bustle around them, it wasn't easy to have a conversation, but they managed a little small talk, mostly about her work and his.

When she finished eating, Shannon sipped her cola while James finished his beer. Setting her plastic tumbler aside, she leaned forward, elbows propped on the table. "Can I ask you a question?"

Something about her tone made his eyebrows rise a little, but he set his drink aside and nodded. "Of course."

"What was it about that watercolor that made you sad?"

He knew exactly which painting she meant, but because her question had caught him by surprise, he stalled for a little time. "Which watercolor?"

Her expression told him she'd seen through his tactic, but she answered patiently, "The one of the rose garden and the watering can. I couldn't see anything about it that seemed particularly forlorn. So why did it made you sad?"

It was so rare for anyone to read emotions he chose to hide and he'd thought he'd hidden his reaction to the watercolor quite well. He wondered if even his closest friends in the study group would have realized that he'd been struck by wistful nostalgia when his eyes had fallen on that simple little painting.

The fact that she saw things in him that other people seemed to miss was only one of the reasons Shannon Gambill continued to intrigue him. "I wasn't sad, exactly. But the painting reminded me of my grandmother. My mom's mother. She loved her roses."

Shannon nodded in comprehension. "You miss her."

"Very much." Sometimes it still surprised him how much random thoughts of her could hurt him.

"How long has she been gone?"

"Almost ten years. I was a senior in college when she passed away."

"I'm sorry. I was very close to my maternal grandmother, too. She died three years ago. My dad's mom lives in St. Louis, and I get to see her a couple of times a year. I love her, but I'm not as close to her as I was to my other grandmother, maybe because Grammy lived here in Arkansas and I saw her all the time."

"I never knew my father's mother. She died before I was born."

She toyed with the straw in her soda glass as she asked, "What did your maternal grandmother give you that no one else did?"

An interesting question. He thought about it for a moment before answering simply, "Fun."

Maybe she interpreted that response a bit more seriously than he'd intended it. Rather than the smile he'd expected, her expressive face reflected concern, and maybe a hint of sympathy. "You didn't have much fun as a child?"

He had no intention of playing poor-me with Shannon—or anyone else, for that matter. No one was interested in attending his pity party, he reminded himself, hearing an echo of his father's voice in his head. "Actually, I had quite a nice childhood. I was an only child and my parents were able to provide me with advantages most kids don't have. Educational and cultural opportunities, extensive travel, that sort of thing."

"You said you'd visited some of the countries we saw represented in that gift shop."

"Most of them," he admitted. "We went on family vacations during spring breaks, Christmas vacations and summers while I was growing up. They wanted me to see as much of the world as possible, especially the countries that are the most culturally and economically different from this one. We toured South and Central America, Asia, Eastern Europe, the South Pacific islands—I never knew where we would spend the next break from school."

He reached for his beer, hoping he hadn't sounded boastful. He didn't want her pity, but he wasn't trying to impress her, either. She'd asked about his childhood and he'd described it candidly. Simple as that.

"So it was just you and your parents on all those trips?"

He nodded, gazing out at the bustling sidewalk to avoid her too-perceptive gaze. "Just the three of us."

"But it wasn't fun."

"I didn't say that."

"Yes," she reminded him gently. "You did."

This date wasn't going exactly as he'd expected. Certainly not the way his dates usually proceeded, with him skillfully leading the conversations in the directions he wanted them to go.

"You said you were an only child," she continued before he had a chance to think of a new topic. "Didn't you have cousins to play with? My family was always getting together with my aunts and uncles and cousins when I was growing up—like my nieces and nephews play with their cousins now."

"I have one cousin, on my mother's side. My mother's sister, Beverly, has a daughter, Kelly. Kelly's quite a bit younger than I am, though—she'll turn twenty in a couple of weeks and I'll be thirty the first week of October—so we weren't really close growing up. She has cystic fibrosis," he added with the tinge of sadness that always accompanied thoughts of his fragile cousin. "Her health is very precarious."

Shannon's expressive green eyes turned to liquid emerald in sympathy. "I'm sorry to hear that. Is she the reason you've considered going into pulmonology?"

He was a little surprised she'd remembered that passing comment. He nodded. "I thought about it, but I've pretty much decided to stick with a pediatric infectious disease specialty."

"Do you see your aunt and uncle and cousin very often? Do they live in this area?"

"My uncle died a few years ago in a car accident. Aunt Beverly and Kelly live an hour south of Little Rock, but they spend quite a bit of time with Kelly's doctors here. I see them occasionally when they're in town, though it's been a few months since we've had a chance to get together."

"Your poor aunt." Shannon's expression was even more sad now. "She's had to deal with a lot of tragedy, hasn't she?"

"Yes, she has."

"Are she and your mother close?"

"Not really. She's several years younger than my mother and—well, Aunt Beverly has never gotten along with my father. So I haven't spent much time with Kelly, especially since our grandmother died and she was just a little girl then."

He hadn't talked about his family or his background so much with anyone, and especially on such short acquaintance. Shannon had a way of finding out things from him that he usually kept to himself. Most people weren't as persistent in penetrating what he thought of as the Stillman family reserve.

"If you're finished, we should probably let someone else have our table," he said, deciding there had been enough dissection of his childhood. "Would you like to go hear some music? The piano bar across the street is always lively."

Though she stood obligingly, she didn't look particularly enthusiastic about his suggestion. "Could we just walk some more, instead? I guess I'm not in the mood for lively tonight."

He wasn't, either, for that matter. They wouldn't be able to talk in a noisy bar and he was enjoying talking to Shannon. But maybe it was time for him to take charge of the conversation, he thought as he walked out of the burrito restaurant beside her. Shannon had a way of leading him into areas he wasn't really comfortable discussing.

He couldn't help wondering if she, too, would rate his communication skills as "needing improvement."

A welcome breeze wafted off the river as Shannon and James strolled the Sculptural Promenade that wound along its bank behind the River Market pavilions. The Junction Bridge, a one-hundred-year-old former railroad bridge that had been converted to a pedestrian walkway over the river to link Little Rock and North Little Rock, loomed ahead of them against the darkening sky, but they weren't interested in climbing the steps or taking the elevator to the top.

With the twin cities skylines spreading on either side of them and a few other couples taking advantage of the perfect weather to stroll ahead and behind them, Shannon and James focused on each other during their walk. Shannon freely admitted she was trying to get to know him better—she wasn't sure what James's goal was. He asked a few questions about her, but they were rather superficial, maybe because he didn't want to encourage her to get too personal with him in return. It seemed to make him very uncomfortable to share too much of himself.

Remembering his vague description of a childhood filled with "educational and cultural" opportunities, but little fun, she suspected that explained why he seemed to be more of an observer than a participant in life. He was pleasant, congenial, very good company—but there was most definitely a wall surrounding his emotions.

"We've talked a lot about my birthday-party business," she said as they leaned against a railing overlooking the flowing river. "Tell me more about doctoring."

He chuckled at her wording. "What do you want to know?"

"Do you like it?"

"For the most part. I haven't actually practiced medicine yet, of course. Not on my own, anyway. Students are closely supervised. But I've seen enough to believe I'll find it a challenging career."

She turned to face him, studying his profile in curiosity. "That's important to you? To be challenged in your career?"

"Of course." He seemed a bit surprised by her question. "Isn't it important to everyone?"

"Not necessarily. Some people like having a job that doesn't require too much of them. A job where they can put in their hours, then leave it all at the office when they go home to their private lives. I doubt that many of those people are drawn to medical careers, though," she admitted.

"You aren't like that or you'd be content with your toy-store job and not interested in starting your own business," James pointed out.

He was trying to direct the conversation to her again, but she wasn't having it this time. "Infectious disease. That's a very challenging specialty, isn't it? Trying to match symptoms with possible diseases?"

He nodded. "The diagnoses are usually evident, but occasionally a more difficult case comes along. Patients who don't show typical symptoms, who don't seem to fit the established checklists."

"Are you the type of person who gets bored easily?"

He shrugged in lieu of an answer.

"Success has always come relatively easily for you, hasn't it? Grades and awards and such, I mean. I mean, you're not even quite thirty and you already have a Ph.D and almost an M.D. I bet that's why you're looking for a career that isn't cut and dried."

He frowned. "I've had to work for the grades and degrees I've gotten. No one gave them to me."

"I didn't say you haven't worked for them. I said they've come relatively easy, especially compared to some people, I'm sure."

He shrugged again.

"So you'll graduate in May. Then what?" she asked. "How long is the residency program for infectious disease?"

"I'll do a three-year pediatrics residency, followed by a three-year fellowship in infectious disease."

"Six years. Wow."

"I'll be practicing medicine during that time, so it's not so bad."

"Will you stay here in Little Rock for those six years?"

"I doubt it. I'll start applying to residency programs in December. I'm submitting applications to programs in several different states. I'll probably return to Arkansas at the end of my residency, though. The children's hospital here is a great place to work."

"I see." So he'd be leaving the state in a few months, for at least six years. This made him even less of a candidate for a long-term relationship. Not that she was looking for anything like that, anyway, she reminded herself hastily. "What are your top choices?"

"I'll spend the month of October doing an away rotation in Seattle, which will give me a chance to look at the program there. In November, I'll be doing an Acting Internship in Boston. I'm also submitting applications to Stanford and Cincinnati and New York and several other programs. I'll probably do my residency at one hospital and my ID fellowship at another, just so I'll have a range of experiences before starting my career practice."

In his own way, James seemed as restless as she, Shannon thought with a flash of insight. She wasn't the traveler he was, but she had sampled several jobs while he tested himself with educational goals.

She'd recently figured out what she was looking for from her career pursuits. A sense of satisfaction. Of accomplishment. Of independence.

What drove James? Why was it so important to him to keep proving himself?

He fascinated her and that meant that maybe he wasn't the only one intrigued by a puzzle.

"So you'll be gone for two whole months?"

He nodded. "I'll leave at the end of this month and be back the first of December."

She nodded and spoke lightly. "Then I'm glad we got to spend this evening together. I've had a very nice time, James."

He glanced down at her. "Does that mean it's over?"

"It's getting late. And I have a party tomorrow evening. I have to start setting up early."

Without protest, he accompanied her to her vehicle. She wondered during that brief, silent walk if he would ask her out again before they parted. Not that he'd asked this time, she reminded herself. This outing had been her idea. But if he did suggest another meeting?

She'd probably agree, she decided on impulse. She enjoyed being with him, and it wasn't as if this was going to lead anywhere, so she didn't have to worry about repercussions. Had she known that from the beginning, it would have made it much easier for her to say yes to his dinner invitations, she mused. Her bruised ego's qualms would not preclude her from having a few good times with a handsome, interesting man as long as they both knew from the beginning it was only temporary. Neither had to worry about being hurt or losing their hard-won independence or…well, or anything like that, she added, knowing exactly which of them suffered from those particular fears.

She pressed her key fob as they approached her car, hearing the loud click as her driver's door unlocked by remote. "So…"

"I had a nice time tonight. I'm glad you suggested the gallery walk, Shannon."

"It was fun."

Other people milled around them in the parking lot and down the more distant city sidewalks. Laughter and conversation, car engines and entangled strains of music, booming bass and trolley bells—all those sounds faded into a muted background as Shannon looked up into James's dark eyes, finding herself suddenly unable to move away. His expression hadn't changed; his features were still schooled into a pleasant smile that could have been directed at anyone. Had he moved nearer to her, or was she the one who'd stopped so close to him? It would take very little effort to place a hand on his chest, just over his heart.

Maybe he saw something in her expression to cue him in to her wayward thoughts. His eyes darkened, and his faint smile faded. Her breath caught in her throat when he leaned his head toward her, closing that short distance…

The cell phone she carried in an outer pocket of her small purse suddenly blasted a raucous chorus of Weird Al's "White and Nerdy," effectively destroying the mood.

Grimacing, Shannon stepped back and fumbled in her purse for the phone, her cheeks warming as she quickly silenced it. "My brother," she mumbled to James, then lifted the phone to her ear. "Hey, Stu, can I call you—"

Her brother interrupted grimly. "Shannon, Kyle's been taken to the children's hospital. He was hit by a car."

Her throat clenched into painful knots. It was all she could do to choke out a few words. "I'm on my way."

Chapter Six

James half expected the entire Gambill family to be gathered in the children's hospital waiting room when he entered behind Shannon. He noted quickly that her many nieces and nephews were absent, which he privately considered a wise call. Other children whined and dashed recklessly through the large, open area filled with couches, chairs and magazine-littered tables, but he'd never considered a hospital lobby a healthy or appropriate environment for kids. He supposed there were times when parents couldn't find other care for their offspring, but Shannon's family seemed to have managed.

At a glance, he identified her parents, Hollis and Virginia, her brother, Stu, her sister, Stacy—the distraught mother—and a uniformed man he'd never met before, whom he assumed to be Stacy's police-officer husband. Only Stu's wife, Karen, was missing—she must be on child-care duty.

The names came easily to him and it was obvious they remembered him, too. Virginia reached out to him immediately, as if greeting a longtime, trusted friend. "James! I'm so glad you're here. We need a doctor's input to help us understand what's going on."

"I was with Shannon when she got the call," he explained, glancing at Shannon, who had her arms filled with her weeping sister. "I followed her here to see if there's anything I can do to help. What happened?"

Virginia's eyes were red and damp, but she seemed to be holding on to her composure for the sake of her family. "Kyle—you remember him—the one you rescued from drowning?"

"I remember."

She blinked rapidly. "He was playing with his in-line skates in their driveway after dinner. It was such a nice evening and he loves playing outside until he absolutely has to come in. Stacy told him to stay away from the street and he said he would. It's a long, smooth concrete driveway, plenty of room for him to skate safely. The twins were playing outside, too, and Stacy felt comfortable leaving them alone while she put the baby to bed. The next thing she knew, the twins were screaming that…that Kyle had been hit by a car."

Overhearing, Stacy pulled away from Shannon with a sob, though she looked as though she were trying to pull herself together. "He wasn't anywhere near the road when I went inside," she insisted. "Baylee said he built a ramp out of some concrete blocks and a piece of plywood he found in the garage. He wanted to do skating tricks. He jumped over the ramp and then couldn't stop himself and he…he…"

"He skated right out into the road and into the path of a car," Hollis finished when his daughter choked on a fresh spate of tears. "He was brought here by ambulance. He was conscious when he came in, and Stacy said he talked a little to her before they sent her and J.P. out here to wait, so we're hoping for the best."

"It's a good thing that he was awake and talking, isn't it, James?" Virginia asked, looking rather pleadingly at him.

"It sounds encouraging," he answered cautiously, though he was reluctant to make any judgments based on what little he'd heard so far.

"He was wearing a helmet and knee pads," Stacy said quickly. "I always make him wear them when he skates or bikes."

Helmets saved many lives, but when a child was hit by a car, a helmet provided only limited protection, James thought with a grimness he didn't want the family to see.

"J.P. got a call from the dispatcher, who had recognized the address," Stu said, nodding toward his somber-looking brother-in-law, whose shock of silver hair stood out from the sea of redheads surrounding him. Despite the hair color, James doubted J.P. was much more than thirty-five. "J.P. got here about the same time as the ambulance. He got to see Kyle for a few minutes with Stacy."

"Where are the other kids?" Shannon asked.

"Our neighbor saw the ambulance and rushed out to see if she could help," Stacy replied wearily, wiping her face with a snowy handkerchief her dad had given her. "She said she'd stay at our house and watch the twins and the baby tonight."

Still looking rattled, Shannon pushed her tumbled red curls from her face and motioned toward her brother-in-law as she glanced up at James. "I guess you've realized this is Stacy's husband, J. P. Malone. J.P., this is James Stillman."

"*Dr.* James Stillman," Virginia correctly quickly. "The man who saved Kyle's life at the lake, J.P."

"Just James." He shook J.P.'s hand, liking the man's agreeably plain face. "I'm a fourth-year med student, not a doctor yet." He saw no need to add that he already had one doctoral degree, so the form of address wasn't technically incorrect.

J.P.'s voice was deep, with a slight country drawl. "I've been wanting to meet you and thank you for what you did for Kyle. The whole family's been talking about the hero they met at the lake."

"What have they told you about Kyle?" Shannon asked before James had to come up with a response. "You said he was talking to you when he arrived?"

Stacy nodded. "J.P. and I were with him until just a couple of minutes before you got here. He didn't say much because they'd already given him something for pain and he was groggy, but he knew who we were. They needed to prep him for surgery, so they told us to wait out here. They said they'd give us regular updates about his progress, but we haven't heard anything yet."

"Surgery?"

"They had me sign a bunch of forms authorizing surgery and blood transfusions, if necessary. There was some internal bleeding," J.P. explained grimly. "He has a broken leg, too, but they said they aren't going to worry about that just yet."

Her face pale with worry, Virginia tugged on James's sleeve. "James, dear, do you think you could go into the operating room and check on Kyle for us?"

"No, ma'am, I can't go into the O.R.," he answered gently. "They'll send someone out with an update as soon as they can. In the meantime, can I get you anything? Coffee? A soda?"

"No, thank you. You're sure you can't go back and check on him? Don't you have an ID or something to show them you're a doctor?"

Shannon sighed. "Mom, he said he can't go back. Don't make him sorry he came with me, okay?"

Virginia frowned. "I just asked."

"It's okay," James murmured to Shannon. "I know she's worried."

"Internal injuries." Stacy, too, looked at James, as if for

reassurance. "That's not always terrible news, right? It could be something minor?"

"I can't really tell you anything without knowing more details," he replied, unwilling to offer possibly false hope. "But the doctors here are the best. Your son is in excellent hands."

Shannon shot him a look, and he couldn't tell if she thought he was saying the wrong things to her family. He could read neither approval nor disapproval in her usually expressive face. What would she have him say? That he was sure her nephew would be fine? He couldn't promise that without knowing the facts, as she must surely understand.

"Isn't there someone you can talk to, James?" Virginia pleaded again.

Feeling the weight of the entire family's gazes upon him, James dug into his pocket for his medical-school ID. "I'll see if anyone I know is on duty in the emergency department," he conceded, clipping the ID to his shirt and wishing he had on the white coat that opened a few more doors for him. "No promises, though—remember, I'm only a med student. And privacy laws prevent them from telling me much, anyway, since I'm not a member of the family."

"You have our permission for them to tell you anything," Stacy assured him fervently.

He didn't think she would be interested at that moment in hearing exactly how the privacy laws worked. Instead, he merely nodded and headed for the ED, wondering what he'd say when he got there.

Shannon frowned at her mother when James disappeared through the waiting room doors. "James came as a friend, Mom, not as a doctor. You shouldn't put him in an awkward position with his coworkers here."

Unfazed by the chiding, her mother simply shrugged. "I'm

sorry, but when it comes to my grandson's care, I'll pull any string I can find. Maybe someone in there will know James and tell him more than we've found out so far."

A hospital volunteer in a cheery blue sleeveless jacket with a photo ID badge pinned to the chest approached the corner of the large, busy waiting lobby where they milled. "Malone family?"

Stacy and J.P. moved forward instantly with the rest of the family crowding behind them. "Yes?" Stacy said eagerly.

The fiftysomething volunteer smiled kindly. "I've been asked to tell you that your son has been taken into surgery. The doctors think it will take about two hours. You'll be given updates every hour and one of the surgeons will talk to you when they've finished. In the meantime, I've just made fresh pots of coffee—both caffeinated and decaf—and there are sodas and snacks in the vending machines. Let me know if there's anything else I can do for you."

"Let's sit down," Shannon suggested, motioning toward an L-shaped arrangement of couches and chairs. She figured they'd better claim seats while they were available. The lobby was getting more crowded. "Mom, are you sure you don't want coffee? I'm going to get some for myself, I can bring you one, too."

Sinking onto the edge of a couch, her mother nodded. "Regular, not decaf. I need the boost."

"Dad?"

He shook his head. "Not right now, thanks, honey." He sat beside his wife, then gazed out the window into the parking lot, lost in his private concern for his grandson.

Stu accompanied Shannon across the room to the coffee station. "Nerve-wracking."

Knowing he referred to the entire situation, she nodded. "Very."

"I think it's a good thing that Kyle was talking to Stacy

and J.P. The helmet probably protected him from head injury. Stacy said the car was moving pretty slowly and the driver was able to apply the brakes before Kyle collided with him."

She tried to take reassurance from his comments, as she knew he intended. "That sounds promising. The fact that he was talking and he recognized Stacy and J.P. surely means there's no head injury."

"Yeah. The doctors will stitch up whatever's bleeding and set the broken leg and he'll be as good as new."

"I'm sure you're right."

Neither of them were certain of anything, Shannon thought somberly, but they had to keep thinking positively. She couldn't bear to imagine any other outcome and she knew it was the same for Stu.

"So how come James was with you tonight?" Stu asked as he poured steaming coffee into two foam cups. "Have you been seeing him since we met at the lake?"

"A couple of times. Just as friends," she said lightly, slipping packets of sugar and creamer into her pocket for her mother. "We did the gallery walk in the River Market tonight, then had dinner at the burrito place. I was just about to head home when you called. James offered to follow me here when I told him what happened, in case there was anything he could do. I'm not sure he expected Mom to nag him into trying to become our personal medical spy."

"He didn't seem to mind, though he's sort of a hard guy to read. Doesn't share what he'd thinking much, does he?"

"Compared to our family, most people are downright reserved," she answered lightly. "Not everyone shares every thought that crosses their minds, the way we tend to do."

"True," her brother acknowledged.

Stu was right, though, Shannon thought as she carefully crossed the room again with a cup of coffee in each hand. James was very reserved. Though he'd seemed concerned about Kyle, he'd been notably reluctant to express any speculation about the boy's condition, optimistic or otherwise. Because he hadn't wanted to offer reassurances that might prove to be wrong? Or—she swallowed hard—because he'd suspected it was worse than they thought?

She gave a cup of coffee to her mother, who set it on the table next to her without tasting it. Shannon sat on the other side of the table and carefully sipped her own hot beverage, though she took little pleasure from the taste. Mostly it just gave her something to do rather than wring her hands.

"There's James," her mom said suddenly, turning on the couch.

Shannon set down her cup and twisted to look in the direction her mother indicated. James was crossing the room toward them, accompanied by a tall, thin woman in a white coat over blue scrubs. Rising to her feet, as were the other members of the family, Shannon searched James's face anxiously, trying to read something…anything…in his tranquil expression.

"Mr. and Mrs. Malone?" the doctor inquired as Stacy and J.P. moved toward her.

Stacy nodded. "Yes?"

"I'm Dr. Luzader, a resident in the emergency department. I saw your son when he was brought in."

"Dr. Luzader was my resident when I rotated through the pediatric ED," James murmured to Shannon. "I told her I was a friend of Kyle's family and she agreed to come out with an update."

"Thank you," she said fervently, squeezing his arm in gratitude before turning back to listen to the doctor.

Dr. Luzader explained that Kyle had been stable when taken into surgery, and that scans had shown no head injuries, which was a good thing. There was some internal bleeding, she said, probably from a lacerated spleen. Surgery would show if any other internal organs were affected.

"He can live without a spleen, right?" Stacy asked, pale but composed now.

"Absolutely," the doctor assured her. "There are some risks of infection afterward, but you'll be instructed about that if he does have to lose the spleen. It could be the surgeons will be able to repair the organ without removing it—it depends on how serious the injury was. The same with any other injuries they might find while they're in there. Once his abdominal injuries have been addressed, the orthopedic team will take care of his broken leg. He'll probably need surgery for that in a day or two, but I don't know that for certain. I'm not an orthopedist."

"So you're saying that Kyle's injuries are not life-threatening?" Hollis asked, a new hope lightening his deep voice.

"There are always some risks following surgery," the doctor answered candidly. "Infection is a concern, but he'll be monitored very closely for the next few days. From what I saw, and barring any complications, Kyle should be fine. Trust me, I've seen much worse injuries come through here, even tonight."

Stacy blinked rapidly against fresh tears. "Thank you so much, Dr. Luzader."

"You're welcome. One of the surgeons will be out to talk to you when they've finished. In the meantime, if you need anything, just ask the hostess, okay? And if you have any questions, maybe young James, here, can answer them," she added with a quick, teasing smile that pushed dimples into her milk-chocolate-colored cheeks and reflected in her dark eyes. "See if he paid attention when he was on my service."

"Thanks, Kayla," he said when she moved to return to her duties.

The doctor wiggled her fingers at him and kept moving.

It felt to Shannon as if the very air were lighter around her and her family after the doctor's brief visit. She hoped they hadn't read too much into the doctor's guarded prediction that Kyle would be fine, but it was such a relief to see optimism returning to her parents' and sister's eyes.

She smiled gratefully at James again. "That helped us all. Thank you."

"We were just lucky I happened to know the resident who saw Kyle. I certainly don't know everyone who works here."

"So Kyle's going to be okay?" Virginia asked James, almost nudging Shannon aside to get closer to him. "That's what the doctor said, right?"

"She said she's seen much worse injuries," he paraphrased. "There's every reason for you to be positive about his prognosis."

Under any other circumstances, Shannon might have been a bit amused by his careful wording. He was in physician mode, she decided, courteous, professional…just a little detached. And while she appreciated what he'd done for them thus far, she would rather he be her friend than the doctor at that moment.

Virginia continued to pelt James with medical questions, and he answered as patiently and thoroughly as if he were taking an oral exam, Shannon mused. He obviously knew his material and was able to explain it clearly enough for her family to understand. But there was still something different about the way he talked when he was being the doctor as opposed to just being James.

She was both fascinated and bemused by the contrast. She always had the sense that there was an invisible wall around his emotions, but the wall became even more opaque when he went into what she was beginning to think of as his "doctor mode." She wondered why. And she wondered if his patients were drawn to his demeanor. Did they find comfort in his obvious competence or were they a bit intimidated by it?

She hadn't even decided which way she felt.

It was almost eleven when the surgery was completed and the family was informed that Kyle was being moved to recovery. The surgeon, a gruff-spoken man with an intriguingly homely face and notably graceful hands, assured them that Kyle was a lucky boy. The injured spleen had been repaired rather than removed, and the other injuries had been limited to contusions and relatively minor lacerations. The broken leg would require surgery, which would be scheduled through the orthopedics department, but that, too, should heal fully with proper care.

Shannon was finally able to draw a deep breath when the surgeon left the family alone again to process what they'd been told. The surgeon had promised to send someone out to get Stacy and J.P. soon so they could join Kyle in recovery before he was transferred to a room for the night.

"Thank heaven," Virginia sighed, her face tired, but her eyes gleaming with relief. She dabbed at her eyes with a tissue, then tossed it in a nearby trash container. "Now if only we can keep him safe long enough to heal."

"I swear, someone's going to have to start watching that boy every single minute," Hollis agreed, the release of tension making him sound gruffer than usual. "It's a miracle he's lived to be eight."

J.P. grimaced ruefully at James. "I had dark hair until Kyle learned to walk," he said, running a hand through his silver mane.

James smiled. "I can believe that."

"His broken leg will heal, right?" Stacy asked James, almost as if she were afraid to believe all would be well. "You don't think he'll have a limp or anything like that, do you?"

Shannon watched as his smile faded instantly into his "doctor look." "The orthopedic surgeons here are very skilled. I've seen them rebuild limbs that were completely shattered. Kyle's in good hands."

Almost exactly the same words he'd used earlier, she recalled. He seemed to have developed certain comments to use in certain situations in his job—like the "in good hands" remark.

Because he always seemed so comfortable making conversation in other situations, she wondered if he was a bit awkward tonight because he was sort of on the sidelines. Not really a family friend, not really a doctor. He'd hinted about leaving a few times while they awaited the outcome of Kyle's surgery—his excuse being that he didn't want to intrude on their family crisis—but each time, there'd been an outcry from the family. Mostly from Virginia, who seemed to believe James was her own personal liaison to the hospital staff, even though he'd done nothing more since finding the emergency-department resident.

Stacy and J.P. were called back to be with their son. Stacy planned to spend the night at the hospital while her husband returned home to their other children. Stu convinced his parents to let him drive them home to rest, assuring them they could come back the next morning to be with their grandson. Lingering long enough to tell her parents good-night, Stacy told Shannon, too, that she should leave.

"We'll be fine here," she promised. "I know you have a party scheduled for tomorrow. You have to fulfill your responsibility or you'll get a reputation as being unreliable."

"The party's not until tomorrow evening," Shannon replied, trying not to take offense at being told how to run her business. Her family was in such a habit of "guiding" Shannon, the youngest child, and she'd been resisting their advice more and more during the past couple of years, but tonight was no time to assert her independence. She supposed Stacy needed something normal tonight, even if that was simply microman-aging her younger sister's affairs.

"I'll come by tomorrow morning," she said, giving Stacy a hug. "Don't worry, I'll have plenty of time to check on Kyle and get ready for the party. Devin's off tomorrow, so she can help me."

"Please don't hesitate to call if there's anything I can do for you," James said to Stacy and J.P. as he made preparations to leave with Shannon. He handed J.P. a card. "My number's on there. I don't have many strings to pull around here, just being a student, but I'll do whatever I can to help if you have any problems or questions."

"Thanks, James." J.P. pocketed the card, nodding at Shannon as if in approval of her friend.

Though James had been unable to find a parking space close to Shannon when they had arrived, he insisted on walking her to her car when they left the hospital. The area was well lit and a security guard in a golf-styled cart passed through occasionally, but James said he wasn't comfortable letting her walk alone through the parking lot at that late hour. Shannon insisted she didn't need the escort, but he just fell into step beside her, anyway, not even listening to her protests that he didn't need to walk so far out of his way.

This only served as more proof of those take-charge tendencies she'd worried about, she told herself. Even if his motives were well-intentioned—as her family's always were—she still disliked the feeling of having her choices dismissed. As if she were a child who needed guiding for her own good.

She knew she was overreacting to his chivalry, even realized that stress and exhaustion were making her overly sensitive, but it still irked.

She pressed her key remote, hearing her car chirp in response as she looked up at James. "Thanks for reassuring my mother this evening. I'm sure the hospital was the last place you wanted to be on a free evening."

"I wasn't able to do much to help."

"Just being there was helpful. The family felt as though they had an interpreter if a medical issue arose that they didn't understand. You did explain a lot to them about the function of the spleen and what they could expect if Kyle had to lose his."

He grimaced a little. "I hope I didn't sound lecturing. Sometimes it's too easy to fall into teaching mode when people ask me medical questions."

Was that genuine self-doubt in his voice? If so, it was the first time she'd heard it from him. "You were great. My mother's ready to adopt you."

That made his smile warm a few degrees. "I'd almost let her. She really is a lovely woman."

"She's a flake."

He chuckled and she knew he'd heard the fondness in her description. "Maybe a little, which only adds to her appeal."

A loaded pause followed the comment, and with the way James was looking at her, Shannon couldn't help wondering what was going through his mind. She had the distinct feeling he was no longer thinking of her mother.

"Drive carefully," he said, reaching around her to open her car door.

She blinked, then nodded. "You, too. Good night, James."

He looked from her eyes to her mouth, then back again. "Good night, Shannon."

He stood where he was and watched her start her car and drive out of the parking lot, as if to make sure she got away safely. Glancing in her rearview mirror as she turned onto the main thoroughfare, she saw him finally turn to walk toward his own parking space.

She lifted one hand off the steering wheel long enough to

touch her lips. Why was it that James had not even touched her, and yet she could so vividly imagine how it would feel to have kissed him good-night?

By Sunday, Kyle's recovery was well underway—so rapidly that the extended family was able to relax and start returning to their own activities. He was expected to remain hospitalized through Wednesday. Shannon wondered if they were keeping him that long mostly to make sure he didn't reinjure himself during those days. Already he'd tried to escape his hospital bed a couple of times because he wanted to explore the hospital. It was no wonder, Shannon thought with the exasperation of a fond aunt, that her poor brother-in-law claimed Kyle was the cause of his prematurely gray hair.

Shannon walked into the hospital room early Sunday afternoon, carrying an electronic toy she'd picked out to keep Kyle entertained during his recuperation, one he could play with without risk of further injury. The boy lay in his bed, his right leg encased in a cast, his red hair tumbled around his face, which was only a shade paler than usual beneath the freckles. J.P. sat on the narrow bed beside him, and together they were reading the Sunday comics from the newspaper. On the other side of the smallish private room, Stacy and their mother sat in the two provided chairs, while their dad leaned against a wide windowsill, gazing out at the Little Rock skyline.

Perching on the end of the bed, safely out of range of her nephew's injured leg, Shannon chatted with her family, learning that Kyle's siblings were spending the day with their uncle Stu and aunt Karen, and that a doctor had been in earlier to inform them that Kyle was making very good progress in his recovery. He was still on track for release in a few days, though it would be another couple of weeks before he'd be cleared to return to school.

"I get a vacation!" Kyle crowed.

His dad leveled a look at him. "Hardly. Your teacher is going to send your work home and your mother and I are going to make sure you don't fall behind."

Kyle heaved a sigh and made an attempt to look pitiful. "But I'm hurt."

"Not so hurt you couldn't beat me at that video game earlier," J.P. retorted, nodding toward the television and gaming system set up in the well-equipped room. "If you're up to racing virtual go-carts, you can do your math and spelling assignments."

Probably knowing that was a discussion he couldn't win, Kyle buried his face in the comics again.

After tapping lightly on the door to announce his arrival, James opened it and peeked in. "Hello. How's the patient today?"

Shannon hoped her family had no way of telling that her pulse rate had just increased at the sight of James's handsome face. Glancing surreptitiously around, she decided in relief and bemusement that they were all too busy being delighted to see him themselves to pay much attention to her. Everyone smiled at him in warm welcome, urging him to come in and visit with them.

She knew he'd been by the day before to check on Kyle, though his visit had not coincided with her own. The family had seemed so pleased by his gesture that one would have thought a celebrity had taken time to visit.

He greeted the others, received a disjointed update on Kyle's condition from parents and grandparents, then turned toward Shannon. "How did your party go yesterday?"

He was the first one to ask. It wasn't that the others didn't care about her business, she assured herself. They were simply preoccupied with Kyle—as they should be. "It went very well, thanks for asking. A dozen six-year-olds at a party with a paleontology theme. I had them dig in boxes of dirt for plastic dinosaur bones, make their own fossil rocks with plaster and play pin the tail on the Brachiosaurus. They ate 'dirt cake' made of chocolate wafer cookies and pudding with gummy dinosaurs on top, and drank 'swamp water,' which was just green-tinted fruit punch. The party hats were plastic pith helmets, and all the party favors were dinosaur-themed. They had a great time, I think."

"That sounds like fun, Aunt Shannon," Kyle said enviously. "I want a dinosaur party."

Stacy lifted an eyebrow. "I thought you said you wanted a superhero party. Or a race-car-driver party."

"I want them all," Kyle agreed with a grin. "You do cool parties, Aunt Shannon."

"Thanks, sweetie." Shannon smiled, then glanced at her watch, suddenly remembering something. "We have those tickets to the play tonight, Stacy. Are you still planning to go with me?"

Stacy wrinkled her nose. "No, I'm just not in the mood tonight, sorry. Maybe Mom would like to use my ticket?"

Their mother shook her head. "Oh, no, I'm much too tired for tonight."

Shannon nodded, figuring she'd have to forfeit the tickets this time, since she couldn't think of anyone else to ask on such short notice. She didn't blame her family for begging off—it had certainly been an exhausting weekend.

"Maybe James can go with you," her mother suggested brightly, looking delighted to have come up with the spur-of-the-moment idea.

"Uh—"

"That would be nice," Stacy agreed, looking eagerly from Shannon to James and back again. "You'd be welcome to my ticket, James, if you're available this evening. You do like dinner theater, don't you?"

"I'm sure James has other plans for tonight, you two," Shannon said repressively. "He's a busy man."

"Actually, I don't have plans for tonight," James corrected rather quickly. "I was just planning to stay in and read, but I'd be happy to accompany you to the play, so your tickets don't have to go to waste."

"They were free, anyway," she said with a slight shrug, self-conscious at having all eyes on her then. "A friend gave them to me when she had a chance to go on a cruise this week instead."

"All the more reason you should get to enjoy them," he replied promptly.

"There you go, honey. James will go with you, so you don't have to miss the play." Her mother looked as though she were mentally patting her own back for making this happen. "I'm sure you'll both have a lovely time."

Looking from her family's smug smiles to James's rather amused expression, Shannon told herself this was probably her own fault. She should have kept her mouth shut about the play.

Chapter Seven

It was after ten when James drove Shannon home from the dinner theater that night. She had suggested they meet at the theater, but he'd gently overridden her that time. It was much more efficient to share a car, he'd pointed out, deciding he'd have better luck with that argument than to voice concerns about her safety leaving the theater well after dark. She had conceded without argument, but he could tell she didn't entirely buy his reasoning.

He had to be at the hospital in less than eight hours, but he was in no hurry to leave her. He'd had a good time with her that evening—as he always did—even though she'd been pretty much railroaded by her family into accepting his company.

It had occurred to him during the evening that his parents would have hated every minute of the outing. The food at the theater had been buffet-style, simple meats and veggies and casseroles aimed to please a variety of tastes, especially the middle-aged and senior citizens who seemed to make up the majority of the patrons. He and Shannon had definitely been among the younger diners. The play that had followed dinner had been a rather silly comedy, and the actors, while talented, had played their parts broadly with frequent winks toward the laughing audience.

"I was surprised you'd never seen that play before," Shannon commented as he turned the car into her driveway. "It's been done by a zillion community theaters and touring productions, and it was made into a 1950s movie musical."

It wasn't the first time she'd expressed surprise that he'd been unfamiliar with the lightweight comedy. "Have you not seen many plays?" she asked, still trying to ferret out the reason.

He shrugged as he put the gear shift into Park. "Yes, quite a few, actually. My parents made sure we attended the theater occasionally while I was growing up. But they wouldn't have appreciated that play. They favored heavily intellectual, metaphorical plays—the bleaker, the better. They hated musicals and were generally disdainful of comedies."

"Ouch. So you were watching Chekov plays as a child?"

"When my parents were in the mood for lighter fare," he answered with a wry chuckle.

"So they placed no value at all on occasional escapism? On simple entertainment?"

"According to Professor Bruce Stillman, Ph.D, contemporary entertainment is nothing more than mental thumbsucking for lazy adults. They don't own a television and their very extensive library is filled with classics and obscure literary tomes. My dad insists the only good fiction is the kind that illuminates, dissects and evaluates. A happy ending is never a sign of quality writing, at least in his exalted opinion."

"Boy, he'd hate my extensive collection of mysteries and romantic-suspense paperbacks."

James chuckled. "Yes, he would. He doesn't know I've become a connoisseur of mysteries and thrillers in the past couple of years. I even watch an occasional scripted television program, though trying to keep up with med-school studies doesn't give me a lot of time to watch TV. My friend Ron has been introducing me to the pleasures of science-fiction films. He's hooked on them."

"So the play tonight must have seemed really silly to you. And the food was hardly gourmet…"

"I had a great time tonight," he interrupted firmly when she seemed to be apologizing for the evening's entertainment. "And I was watching the other people in the theater with us. Some of those older audience members were laughing so hard they were having to wipe tears from their eyes. Unlike my father, I see nothing wrong with people escaping their problems for a few hours to enjoy laughing with their friends. Since I've become close to my study-group friends, I've learned to appreciate the value of laughter to mitigate stress and anxiety."

"To mitigate stress and anxiety?" she repeated in a murmur.

He frowned, not quite certain how to interpret her tone.

Maybe he'd told her too much. He didn't usually share so many details about his childhood with his pedantic parents. He certainly hadn't been angling for sympathy—he'd told her before that his past had been one of privilege, certainly not deserving of pity. Instead, he'd wanted to give her a little glimpse into his past so she could understand him a little better, something that was becoming increasingly important to him.

He really was lousy at this communication thing, he thought glumly.

She reached for the bag sitting by her feet. "It's getting late and I know you have to work early."

He glanced at the house, which was dark except for one dim light shining through what he assumed was the living room window. "Has your housemate already gone to bed?"

"No, Devin's working tonight. We usually try to leave enough lights on to make people think someone's home. Guess she forgot tonight. She runs late sometimes and gets kind of scatterbrained."

He reached for his door handle. "I'll walk you to the door."

"That's not—"

He was already sliding out of the car. He knew Shannon didn't like to be overruled, but he wanted to make sure no one was lurking in the bushes or waiting inside the darkened house, paranoid though that sounded. His father would probably attribute his heightened imagination to the thrillers he'd been reading lately. Remembering one particularly gruesome scene he'd read only a couple nights before, he moved closer to Shannon as she dug in her purse for her door keys.

She unlocked her door by the illumination of the softly glowing porch light, then turned to him with lifted eyebrows. "Okay, I'm safely home. Are you satisfied?"

He glanced down at her with a faint smile. "Not by a long shot."

Her lashes lowered, then swept back up so that she met his gaze squarely. "I'm not inviting you in. This time."

"I didn't expect you to," he replied equably, though he made note of her addendum. He liked the possibility that there would be a next time—and that there was a chance it would end a bit differently than this one.

"I like being with you, James. You…intrigue me."

"I thought you said I made you nervous. And wary."

"All of the above," she replied, sounding amused. "Which makes it even more interesting spending time with you."

Taking encouragement from her smile, he leaned his head toward hers. "I enjoy being with you, too, Shannon."

She planted a hand on his chest, holding him an inch away from making contact with her lips. "Just so you know…I'm not looking for anything long-term. I'm not interested in that right now. After two failed relationships before I even turned twenty-five, I want to concentrate on just leading my own life for a while."

He nodded. "I got that idea, already. And I'm not planning to disrupt your life. After all, I'll be out of the state for two of the last three months of this year, then leaving again in May to pursue a six-year residency."

"So you're just looking to have a little fun while you finish your last year of school?"

He wouldn't have put it that way, exactly, but he supposed it was close enough. "Sure."

Apparently, it was enough to put Shannon more at ease with him. After a momentary pause, she dimpled up at him. "Okay. Personally, I think you need to have a little fun before you dive into your residency."

His attention focused on her smile. His mind swirled with disjointed images of some of the fun he could have with her, and his body responded uncomfortably to those mental pictures. It had definitely been too long since he'd had, um, fun.

Taking him by surprise, Shannon curled her fingers around his shirt, drawing him toward her rather than holding him off this time. She rose on tiptoes and pressed a quick kiss to his mouth.

"Thanks for going with me tonight, James," she said as she drew away. "I enjoyed it."

He caught her shoulders and lowered his head to steal a more thorough kiss. "Good night, Shannon," he said rather gruffly when he forced himself eventually to break away, far from satisfied but knowing when to quit. For now.

Her expression flatteringly dazed, she cleared her throat. "Um—g'night," she muttered and fumbled quickly with the door. She closed it between them with a loud snap.

Smiling a little, James turned and walked back to his car, knowing he would see her again soon.

Shannon almost dreaded the visit with her nephew Monday afternoon. Though she wanted to see Kyle, she suspected she would be grilled by her other family members about her outing with James. She refused to call it a date since it hadn't been either her idea or his to attend the play together—they'd let themselves be persuaded by her matchmaking mom.

She wished her family could understand that she was perfectly content being single for now. They seemed to think her heart had been broken by Greg and then Philip, and that she needed to be nudged back into the dating scene by her well-meaning loved ones. She'd tried but apparently failed to convince them that both of those relationships had left her with more bruises than breaks.

Yes, Greg had dumped her, but to be honest, she'd already been considering breaking that ill-advised teenage engagement. In hindsight and with the wisdom gained from a few more years of living, she saw now that the betrothal had been spurred as much by their other high-school friends getting engaged as by a true desire on her part to tie herself to Greg for the rest of her life. She had indulged in youthful fantasies of a white-lace wedding, but the thought of the marriage that would follow had given her concern even then. Greg had simply made the decision for them both while she'd been dithering about how to break the news to him without hurting him too badly—which seemed ironic now.

As for Philip, her family seemed to forget that she was

the one who had ended that relatively brief relationship. It had never progressed to the engagement stage. He hadn't considered her properly groomed yet to be the wife of a socially-conscious dentist. He'd expressed concerns about the independent streak she'd been cultivating even then, and about her stubbornness when she made up her own mind about what was best for her. Her outspokenness was something else he'd criticized. He'd advised her only half-teasingly on several occasions to let an occasional thought go unvoiced—especially if it involved any sort of criticism of him.

She could see now that she was lucky to be free of both of them—and that she'd gained that freedom while still young and otherwise unencumbered—but her marriage-and-children-obsessed family were convinced she would be better off with someone to "take care of her." She supposed it was the fate of the youngest child to always be seen as somewhat dependent or in need of protection. Even though she'd been making it on her own for some time now.

She walked into the boy's room with a bright smile pasted on her face and a colorful, spaceship-shaped Mylar balloon bobbing above her head. She'd just gotten off work at the toy store and she'd picked up the balloon on her way out.

"Cool, thanks, Aunt Shannon!"

She kissed her nephew's cheek, then tied the balloon to the bedrail where he could see it floating above him. "You're welcome."

"Well…?" her mother asked eagerly.

Her mother and Stacy were the only other visitors at the moment. Shannon turned to them with her hands on her hips and a firm set of her jaw. "The food was good, the play was cute, and James and I had a very nice time. He took me home, walked me to my door and that was the end of it, okay? I really see no need to analyze every minute, as I'm sure the two of you are just itching to do."

"Did he kiss you good-night, Aunt Shannon?"

Her jaw dropping, Shannon whirled toward the bed. She'd hoped at least her nephew would be more interested in something other than her social life! "Holy kamoley, Kyle—"

But Stacy and their mother were laughing now, so maybe Kyle's teasingly naive question had been a good thing.

"That, young man, is none of your business," Shannon said, touching a fingertip to her nephew's up-tilted nose. Quickly changing the subject, she looked at her sister. "What did the doctors say today?"

She was sure that Stacy would have liked to ask more about the evening with James, but maybe because of Kyle's avid listening, Stacy allowed herself to be diverted. Kyle's medical reports were excellent and he was still expected to leave the hospital Wednesday morning. Stacy would have her hands full taking care of him and the baby. J.P. would pitch in when he wasn't at work, and the twins were old enough to help out quite a bit around the house, which Shannon knew they did. Their mother would help, too, so Shannon wasn't too worried about her sister, though Stacy would expect plenty of sympathy during the next few weeks.

A tap on the door made Shannon's pulse rate jump. She chided herself for her overreaction. There was no way she could recognize a simple knock on the door, she told herself... and yet, somehow, she had.

James stuck his head into the room with a smile. "How's it going in here?" he asked.

He wore a white coat over a blue dress shirt, blue patterned tie and gray pants. She recognized a stethoscope and reflex hammer sticking out of one of his pockets, while other pockets held pens and notepads and what appeared to be sheets of folded papers. A plastic photo ID clipped to his collar identified him as a medical student.

Though she'd seen his "doctor face" before, this was the

first time she'd actually seen him wearing the uniform. And she had to admit, it intimidated her just a little, though she couldn't have explained exactly why. She was intensely aware of her own work uniform—the khaki slacks and white shirt all the toy-store employees wore beneath the bright green apron required while working the floor. She felt a little disheveled compared to James, but there was nothing unusual about that.

He gave her one of his faint smiles and her uncharacteristic attack of timidity transformed into something entirely different. In that moment, he was the man who had kissed her on her doorstep, who had caused her a few hours of sleeplessness last night as she'd replayed that embrace over and over in her mind. Who'd have thought the reserved, well-mannered and enigmatic doctor would kiss like *that?*

She felt her cheeks warm a little and she looked quickly away, hoping no one else noticed.

Her mother was notably not intimidated by James's white coat. She beamed at him. "Well, don't you look nice today. Are you working here in the children's hospital?"

"I have been," he replied lightly. "I'm doing a pediatric infectious disease rotation. I got off work a little early today."

"Infectious disease?" Stacy looked nervously from James to Kyle.

James shook his head reassuringly. "Don't worry, we take many precautions against contamination. For example, I used the disinfectant foam on the wall outside this room before entering—as you should all be doing when you come in."

Assuring him they were diligent in using the foam, Stacy then launched into a word-by-word account of everything any of the medical staff had said to her since she'd last seen James, searching his face while she talked as if to judge his reactions.

He responded patiently to all questions, answering with the

caution she'd noticed before, responding candidly but without a great deal of elaboration. No airy assurances, no expounding to show off his knowledge, no stepping beyond the boundaries of his limited expertise. Her family might consider him their own personal medical expert, but James treated them with the respectful civility of a near-stranger whenever he was being asked to respond as a doctor rather than a friend.

As handsome and impressive as he might be as James-the-physician, she missed the warmth in his dark eyes and the elusive half-smile of her friend. She broke into the conversation as quickly as she could, deliberately directing the topic away from medicine. "I had a funny thing happen at work today. You'll probably all get a laugh out of it."

She wasn't entirely sure—he was so darned hard to read—but she thought James was relieved by the diversion. "I'd like to hear it," he said, turning toward her. "What happened?"

She told them about the adorable elderly couple who'd come to the store to purchase a video-game system that afternoon, asking for Shannon's help because they had no familiarity with video gaming. They'd implied at first that they were buying the system for a grandchild, but when she'd asked questions to determine the child's age and gaming experience, the woman had admitted that they were really buying the system for themselves.

"We've been watching all those commercials on the television," she had explained, "and it just looks like all those people are having so much fun. Ernie and I want to play, too. We get tired of staring at each other all afternoon and I just don't think I can stand another game of gin rummy."

Shannon had spent the next hour happily playing demo games with the couple, showing them how the different systems operated and some of the games available for each one. They had learned quickly and after bickering amusingly for a while, they'd finally settled on the system that would incorporate healthy exercise into the games of bowling, tennis and golf that had most intrigued them.

"Old people wanted to play video games?" Kyle asked in astonishment. "Did you show them the new *Warriors from Beyond the Realm* game, Aunt Shannon? That one is so sweet."

Shannon laughed and shook her head. "I don't think they're interested in sword fights and laser-gun battles, Kyle. Though they said they'd be back to look at more sports games once they've mastered the ones they bought."

"Well, frankly, I'd rather play gin rummy," Shannon's mother asserted. "I don't care for video games myself."

"My friends Ron and Connor and I often played video games during study breaks to clear our minds and relax a little before hitting the books again," James said.

Was there a touch of wistfulness in his voice? Stacy wondered if she was the only one to notice. Just from the little he had told her, she sensed that James missed those long study sessions with his friends, though he'd told her he didn't miss all the lectures and tests of the first two years of medical school. She suspected he would miss his friends very much when they went their separate ways after graduation. If he had friends outside of medical school, he hadn't mentioned any during their conversations. He talked about Ron and Haley and Connor and Anne as if he'd known them all his life.

He glanced at his watch. "I missed lunch today because I got caught up in a consult. Frankly, I'm starving. Can I tempt you ladies with a snack in the hospital cafeteria? My treat, I get a discount."

Shannon's mother smiled at him warmly, giving Shannon another one of those this-guy-is-wonderful-hang-on-to-him looks. "Thank you, dear, but Hollis, Stu and Karen are supposed to arrive soon. Stu and Karen are going to sit with Kyle while Hollis and I go out for a bite. Then I'm going to spend the night with Kyle so Stacy can go home to her husband and their other children for a few hours. J.P. has taken a few days off to help out here and at home."

The family was making sure Kyle wasn't left alone in the hospital room for more than an hour or so at a time, even though they knew the staff was vigilant in taking care of him. But Kyle's loved ones knew how much trouble the boy could get into even lying in the bed with a broken leg and a surgical scar, Shannon though wryly. She'd offered to spend one night with the boy, but this was the first time Stacy had been persuaded to leave and their mother had insisted on staying tonight. She suspected Stacy would stay again Tuesday night. They would all be relieved for Stacy's sake when Kyle went home on Wednesday.

Four kids—one in diapers, one in a cast. Shannon shook her head, thanking the stars for her own relatively carefree independence. She wasn't sure she could deal with all these crises even as well as Stacy, who was admittedly excitable under the best of circumstances, but always came through admirably when she had to.

"Shannon, you could keep James company while he eats," Stacy prodded. "I'm sure you're hungry, too. You're always hungry," she added with a somewhat tired laugh.

Shannon had half expected that suggestion from her mom. Now her sister was in on the matchmaking. She leveled a quick frown at Stacy. "Since the two of you have other plans, I'd imagine that James would rather eat somewhere other than the hospital cafeteria. You certainly don't have to hang around here for our sake, James."

"And neither do you, Shannon," Stacy answered promptly. "I know Kyle appreciates your visit, but he'll have Stu and Karen here with him until Mom and Dad get back from dinner. You've had a long day at work. Go relax for a while."

"That's an excellent suggestion," their mother agreed.

"You've been on your feet all day at the toy store and you have to work again tomorrow. There's no need to spend your few hours off sitting here in a hospital room."

As if to reinforce their arguments, a nutrition-services aide entered the room just then with Kyle's dinner on a tray. Stacy immediately busied herself helping her son sit up in the bed so he could eat. Their mother hovered, too, coaxing the boy to eat his vegetables so he could quickly regain his strength.

"I didn't intend to put you in an awkward position or take you away from your family," James murmured to Shannon while the rest of the family was occupied. "I'd be delighted for you to join me for dinner, but only if you want to."

Annoyed with all of them—and maybe herself, as well—she reached for her purse. "Actually, I'm headed home. I put some ingredients in the slow cooker this morning so I'd have dinner ready this evening. There's enough for you, too, if you want to follow me," she added a bit gruffly. "If not, then I'll see you later."

She was well aware that it wasn't the most gracious invitation; she didn't need the chiding looks from her mother and sister to drive the point home. But James merely nodded. "Thanks, that sounds great."

Shannon kissed her nephew's cheek, told him she would see him the next day, then said good night to her mother and sister with a bit less warmth. Judging from their expressions, they knew exactly why she was annoyed at them—but the satisfied looks they exchanged proved they weren't particularly repentant.

It was earlier than Devin usually left for work, but she was already gone by the time Shannon walked in with James following behind her. She had left a note taped to the slow cooker. "Smells delish, but meeting friends for pizza before work. Last-minute plan. Save the leftovers!"

Having expected Devin to join her and James for dinner, Shannon hid a sudden, nervous qualm when she turned to him with a fake smile. "Looks like it's just the two of us. I'll make a quick salad and heat some bread. Dinner will be ready in about fifteen minutes, if you want to wash up and watch the news or something while I finish up in here."

"Anything I can do to help?"

"No, thanks. The kitchen's kind of small for two. Make yourself comfortable in the living room. The TV's behind the cabinet door."

He nodded and turned to leave the room. She drew a deep breath when she was alone in the small, galley-styled kitchen. Being in such close quarters with James was definitely not conducive to clear thinking, she mused as she pulled wheat rolls out of the freezer and salad makings from the fridge.

At least the house was tidy, even though they hadn't been expecting company. She and Devin always kept the living room ready for guests and both tended to be neat in other areas, as well.

She wondered what James thought of their little rent house—which led her to wondering where and how he lived. Though they had seen each other in their work environments, they hadn't glimpsed much of each other's private lives yet. Bringing James into her home felt like another step forward in their...well, she would call it friendship, because that was a comfortable and uncomplicated term. Even though her feelings for James were rarely comfortable and almost never uncomplicated.

When the simple meal was ready, she set the serving dishes on the table in the tiny dining area at the end of the narrow kitchen, then went in search of James. Rather than watching television, he had entertained himself looking through the party albums displayed on what they generously referred to as their conference table, even though it barely seated four comfortably. The albums held photos of all the parties she had organized, along with samples of invitations, catalogs of party favors and decorations, theme descriptions, options and price lists.

As proud as she was of her work and of the materials she had assembled to promote her business, she still felt a little self-conscious when James looked up at her. She wanted his reaction to what he'd seen to be positive, but not patronizing. She hated being patted on the head like a kindergartner displaying prized crayon artwork.

"I hope you don't mind that I looked through your albums."

She shook her head. "Of course not. I told you to make yourself at home. And those albums are there for visitors to look through—most of the stuff in them is also available at my Web site."

"Yes, I've seen your site. It's an excellent sales tool. There are more photos in your albums, though. I enjoyed looking at them. The parties look like fun. I'm sure the guests had a great time at all of them."

"That was the goal. Dinner's ready, by the way."

"It smells delicious."

"You haven't even asked what we're having."

He shrugged. "Doesn't matter. I'm not a picky eater. And I'm hungry enough to eat dirt soup tonight."

She laughed. "It's not quite that bad. I made Santa Fe chicken. Chicken, black beans, tomatoes and green chilies. Salad and wheat rolls on the side."

"Sounds much better than dirt soup," he agreed eagerly.

Laughing again, she led him to the table.

He helped himself to a generous portion of the dish, topping it with the sour cream and grated cheese she'd provided for garnish. They talked about her work while they ate and she made him laugh several times with amusing anecdotes from some of her parties.

She loved hearing him laugh, she thought with a little tingle of pleasure. Just as she loved seeing him eating her meal with such obvious pleasure. She loved seeing him looking relaxed and comfy at her table, more approachable now that he'd shed his white coat and tie, turning back the sleeves of his blue dress shirt to reveal his nice forearms. She loved...

Choking a little on a bite of chicken, she pushed any further thoughts along that line to the back of her mind. She didn't even know James that well, she reprimanded herself. There was no need to get carried away here.

Chapter Eight

"Your parties sound great," James said as he helped Shannon clear away the dishes after the meal, coordinating their movements in the tight space to keep from stumbling into each other. She did a few quick sidesteps to keep from brushing against him as she loaded the dishwasher, her pulse racing a little more each time they accidentally made contact.

"I have a feeling your business is going to be very successful once you get more fully established."

Trying to keep her thoughts focused on the conversation and the task at hand, she replied, "I hope you're right. My family keeps warning me that it's difficult to make a living in a small business venture like mine."

He shrugged. "Lots of people make a living running their own businesses. With enough passion and enough hustle, there's no reason you can't make a success of it. And you seem to have both."

She beamed at him. "Thank you. That's exactly the way I feel about it. Passionate and willing to hustle."

"It shows," he assured her.

She found herself staring at his smiling lips as she asked, "Would you like some dessert?"

"No, thank you. That second roll filled me up."

"Coffee?"

"No, I'm good, thanks."

She wasn't quite sure what to do with him if she wasn't feeding him. She motioned toward the living room. "We could sit and talk for a little while before you go. We've been talking about my day all evening. I'd like to hear about yours."

He blinked, as if surprised that she'd be interested in his work. Was it really so rare for anyone to ask about his day? Sure, he was single and lived alone, but didn't he talk to his friends? His parents?

He followed her into the living room and took a seat beside her on the couch. "What would you like to know?"

She sighed. "Don't put on your doctor face, I don't have any medical questions. I just wondered how your day went. Did anything funny happen? Do you like your rotation? Are you still interested in pursuing infectious disease training or do you like pulmonology even more now?"

He frowned, focusing on one particular phrase she had used rather than the question she'd asked. "My doctor face?"

"Yes. Hasn't anyone mentioned that you have a different expression when you're in physician mode than when you're being just-James?"

"Um. No, not exactly. I'm not sure what you mean."

She waved a hand in a vague gesture. "You just look different when you're on the job. I can't explain it, exactly. You're sure no one else has said anything?"

"Well…"

"They have, haven't they?"

Looking a little uncomfortable, he shrugged. "Not exactly in those words. But I've been told my communication skills could use some improvement, which to be honest, I don't understand. I've never had any trouble talking with people. I don't feel uncomfortable talking to patients or their families. They usually seem to understand what I've told them, they seem satisfied I know what I'm doing, but when they have questions or problems, they tend to wait to tell someone else rather than bringing it up with me."

She tilted her head, studying him closely. "Have you talked about this with your study friends?"

He shifted a little uncomfortably. "No. There's not a lot to discuss, really. I've gotten pretty good evaluations, for the most part, just an occasional comment that my communication could use some work."

She suspected he hadn't mentioned the critique to his parents, either, since he didn't seem to be particularly close to them from what she had gathered. Didn't James have anyone to turn to when he had a problem?

And there she went feeling a little sorry for him again, she thought with a slight shake of her head. Which was ridiculous, considering most people would have thought he led just about the perfect life.

"I'm sure you're an excellent doctor, James," she said gently. "In fact, I know you are. I've sort of seen you on in that light a couple of times. I'd trust any member of my family into your care—and my mother and sister are ready to hang a halo over your head because you've been so thoughtful and helpful with Kyle."

She was secretly amused by the faint hint of color that appeared then disappeared almost as quickly on his lean cheeks. "I haven't really done anything for Kyle. Just checked in on him a couple of times."

"Which means a lot to them."

"So what did you mean when you told me not to put on my 'doctor face'?"

She hesitated a moment, then shrugged. "Like I said, you're a bit different when you're presenting yourself as a doctor. You get a little more serious, a little more formal in your speech. Don't get me wrong, you're still polite and pleasant, but you're a bit...well..."

"What?"

"Intimidating."

His eyes widened and she could tell the term took him aback.

"Which could explain why your patients save their questions for someone else," she added. "Maybe they think you don't have time for minor issues or questions. I've had doctors like that in the past. They just seemed so busy and so distracted that I hesitated to bother them with questions or complaints."

He shook his head, obviously bothered by her comments. "I hope you're wrong about that. I've certainly never tried to intimidate anyone."

She rested a hand reassuringly on his arm. "I'm sure you haven't. You just seem so confident and knowledgeable. Those are hardly criticisms."

He didn't look particularly reassured. "Those same two words have been used to describe my father. I've spent my entire adult life trying not to turn into him."

She patted his forearm. With a slight laugh, she said, "It's common enough for a man to want to distinguish himself from his dad—just as many women vow never to turn into their mothers. Doesn't mean we don't love them—we just want to establish our own personalities."

He shook his head. "You haven't met my father, so you can't quite understand—but trust me, my dad goes to great lengths to intimidate people with his superior intelligence.

I'm not trying to establish my independence by trying to act differently. I'm trying to treat other people with more respect than he does."

The more she heard about James's father, the more she suspected she wouldn't like him. She was beginning to understand James a little better, though there were still many facets of him that were a mystery to her—all of them fascinating.

"Then you've succeeded," she said loyally. "You have always been respectful of me and of my family, which is why we all like you so much."

It occurred to her that she was still clutching his bare arm beneath the rolled-up sleeve of his shirt. The warmth of his skin penetrated her palm, heating her blood. She felt a muscle flex beneath her hand, as if he, too, had suddenly become aware of the contact.

He covered her hand with his other hand, giving her fingers a little squeeze. "I like you, too," he said, his voice suddenly sounding a half octave deeper.

Her heart stuttered over a couple of beats. *Like,* he had said. He liked her. A perfectly innocuous and friendly statement, certainly nothing that should make her pulse leap this way. Hadn't she just told him that she liked him, too? It was ridiculous for her to feel this schoolgirl breathlessness over such an innocent comment.

And yet there was nothing innocent about the gleam in his eyes when they lowered slowly from her own, pausing to study her mouth as if memorizing the contours. As if he were mentally replaying the one brief kiss they had shared. At least, that was what she was doing. She could almost taste him again now—which only fueled her hunger for another sample.

She wasn't sure which of them leaned forward first. Maybe the movement was simultaneous. Their lips met with no hesitation on either part, no fumbling or surprise.

Somehow her arms were around his neck. Somehow his were around her back. And she was draped half across his lap, feeling the warmth of him surrounding her, the strength of him against her. Feeling his body's reaction to the embrace, which only intensified her own.

Maybe James had a little trouble expressing himself in words. Maybe he'd been trained too well during his childhood to keep his deepest emotions hidden. But he was certainly communicating very clearly now. She had no trouble at all determining what he wanted. Probably because she wanted the same thing.

She drew her head back a couple of inches to study his face when the kiss ended. He met her gaze openly, making no effort to hide his desire, nor his willingness to leave the next step up to her.

She should send him on his way. They'd known each other only a month—not exactly a long time. They had already implicitly agreed the relationship wouldn't be a lasting one. In only two weeks, he'd be leaving town for two months, after which, who knew if she would ever see him again?

"You still make me nervous, James," she said on a slight sigh.

"But in a good way," she added when his brows drew into a frown. "Mostly."

His beautiful, skilled mouth twitched. "And you still confuse the hell out of me. In a good way. Mostly."

She could resist flattery. Persuasion. Even pleading. But she found James's gentle teasing downright irresistible.

She simply had to taste that little smile again. She planted her mouth against his, winding her fingers in the thick, dark hair at the back of his head. James responded instantly, his lips parting to deepen the kiss, stealing any coherent thought from her mind. A shift of his weight, and she lay half-beneath him on the thick-cushioned sofa. A throw pillow tumbled unheeded to the floor—she swept another out of the way as she snuggled into him.

Their legs tangled as their mouths met, separated, met again, tongues dueling, exploring. James's hand was hot against her stomach beneath her white top. She arched into him, filling his palm with her aching breast, feeling his fingers moving over the thin covering of her white cotton bra. For only a moment, she wished she were wearing something a little more exotic beneath her plain work uniform, but James seemed pleased enough with what he saw when he swept her top over her head.

His mouth sought out the pounding pulse in her neck and at the base of her throat, then slid lower to send her pulse rate soaring even higher. She gasped at the first feel of his tongue and teeth against her sensitized breast, but her hands urged him not to stop the exquisite torment.

He lifted his head and his eyes were enchantingly glazed. She loved knowing she was the reason for that dazed and unfocused look. "Um—maybe I should...?"

"You should stay," she murmured, stroking his cheek with one unsteady hand. "Let's go to my room."

He hesitated only long enough to search her face with one sweeping glance—maybe proving to himself that she had no doubts. Since there were no doubts for him to see—none she allowed herself to show him, anyway—he smiled and rose, holding out a hand to help her up.

"Don't get up." James pressed a hand on Shannon's shoulder as he leaned fully dressed over the bed to kiss her goodbye. "It's late. Go back to sleep."

At least he hadn't left without letting her know, she thought, blinking up at his silhouette against the dim light from the window behind him. She'd have hated waking up to find herself in an empty bed without having heard him leave.

"What time is it?"

"A little after midnight. I have to be at the hospital early, so I'm going home to get some sleep first."

Clutching the sheet in front of her, she reached up to kiss him again. "Be careful going home. And have a good day tomorrow."

"I will, and thanks, you, too. I'll talk to you tomorrow."

Peering into the shadows, she watched him leave the room. She listened as the front door closed behind him, then heard his car start and fade down the street. Only then did she close her eyes again, nestling into the sheets that were still warm from his body.

Maybe there would be second thoughts tomorrow, but for tonight, she was too sleepy and satisfied to care.

Devin was waiting in the living room when Shannon stumbled in the next morning, red hair still damp from her shower. She was buttoning the white shirt she wore with her work khakis, and she'd donned just enough makeup to make her presentable for the day. She had about half an hour to make and eat her breakfast and head for the toy store, she thought with a glance at her watch.

She looked up to find her housemate sitting in a chair, slowly waving a white shirt in one hand. It was the shirt Shannon had worn yesterday—the one James had tossed onto the floor the night before.

"So…"

Shannon cleared her throat. "Um, so that's where I left that."

"I emptied the dishwasher before I left yesterday. And yet I noticed that there were two plates, two glasses, two forks and two knives in there this morning. And a good portion of our slow-cooker meal was gone—either you were very hungry or you had company last night."

"James joined me for dinner last night."

"I have a feeling that's not all he joined you for," Devin murmured.

Shannon cocked an eyebrow and sailed past her toward the kitchen, from which the aroma of coffee wafted temptingly. "Have you had anything to eat?"

Devin followed her into the kitchen, tossing the telltale shirt over the back of a chair. "I had a candy bar. I'll have some of that leftover chicken after I've grabbed a few hours of sleep."

"You should eat something healthier than a candy bar. That's not exactly good for you."

"Speaking of things that aren't good for you…"

Pausing with a box of oatmeal in her hand, Shannon leveled a look at her friend. "Instead of trying to be clever, how about just telling me what's bugging you?"

Devin shrugged. "I've been asking around a little about your new boyfriend."

"James isn't my boyfriend," Shannon denied automatically.

Devin glanced meaningfully at the white shirt, making Shannon flush a little, then turn quickly toward the cabinets to pull out a breakfast bowl. "Why have you been asking about him, anyway?"

"Just curious. I mean, it seemed like you fell kind of hard and fast for the guy. I just wanted to make sure he wasn't another Philip, you know? Another jerk doctor."

"Philip was a dentist."

"You know what I mean."

Scowling, Shannon slammed a spoon onto the counter. "Since when do we check up on each other's friends? Despite the disaster with Philip—which I eventually handled on my own, by the way—I'm quite capable of deciding who I should spend time with. You of all people know how I feel about others interfering in my life, even if it's for my own good. Maybe especially if it's for my own good," she added in a grumble.

"I know, and I wasn't trying to check up on him exactly," Devin assured her hastily. "I was just curious if anyone around the hospital knew anything about him, since I haven't met him."

She really didn't want to ask, but she was unable to resist. "So? What did you hear? What makes you think James isn't good for me?"

"Turns out he dated Elissa Copeland last year. She's a pharmacy student, and she's a friend of Nicki Pearl, who's one of the nurses I work with a lot."

Shannon nodded to show she had followed the connections. "So he dated a pharmacy student. What's the big deal? Did he break her heart or something?"

"Well, no, from what I heard he just bruised her ego a little. She kind of had her heart set on snagging a rich doctor and he made it clear he wasn't interested in anything long-term."

Shannon moistened her lips. "That's not a problem. Neither am I. James and I have already agreed we're just having fun for now."

And he'd been awfully quick to agree, she remembered. She'd sort of thought the firm stipulation had been her idea. Had he encouraged her to believe that?

"And anyway, he's a medical student, not a full doctor," she added. "He won't graduate until May and then he's got six years of residency ahead of him before he's ready to start his own practice."

"Yeah, well, let's just say he doesn't have to worry about paying his bills while he completes his training. I doubt that he even had to take a loan to go to medical school, and you know almost all of them are on loans at least to some extent."

Reluctant as she was to speculate about James's money, Shannon argued, "His parents are both college professors. I'm sure they do okay, but..."

"He hasn't mentioned his grandfather?"

Something about Devin's tone made Shannon pause before replying, "Um...no. He said something about his maternal grandmother."

"His maternal grandfather invented some sort of doohickey that's used in manufacturing equipment all over the world. He doesn't talk about it, apparently, but Elissa did some research on his family and she told Nicki, who mentioned it to me when I asked if anyone knew James."

Her expression conspiratorial now, she added, "They think that's why he's not interested in tying himself down to anyone. I mean, he's good-looking and rich and he's going to be a respected doctor, so why limit his options when he's still so young? He's only in his thirties, after all. Nicki and Elissa didn't know why he wants to work so hard to become a doctor, when he could probably live comfortably without doing much of anything."

"He won't be thirty until next month. And James doesn't strike me as the type to spend his life doing nothing. He already has one advanced degree, and now he's working toward his M.D., preparing to take on a very challenging residency. Whatever his social or financial standing, he works very hard."

Devin held up both hands in response to Shannon's tone. "I just thought you'd want to hear what I found out about him. I mean, I've never thought some rich playboy doctor would be your type."

"James is hardly a playboy doctor. He doesn't brag about his circumstances—just the opposite, actually. This is the first I've heard of a rich grandfather. And I sincerely doubt he's had time to party all that much and still be at the top of his medical-school class, not to mention having earned a Ph.D first."

"You're very defensive about him." Devin studied her quizzically. "You sound like you're getting annoyed with me for telling you these things. Now you know why I said you've fallen hard and fast. Why I'm worried you're going to get hurt again."

"I'm annoyed because you've been gossiping about my friend at the hospital where he works. I would be just as annoyed with anyone who gossiped about you. I'm annoyed because you're treating me as if I'm some dimwit who has to be protected from my own feelings. Philip did not leave me brokenhearted and vulnerable—I dumped his pompous butt. And I decide what sort of relationship I'll have with James, or any other man in my future."

It wasn't the first spat she'd had with Devin—not even the first based on Devin's habit of wanting to watch over Shannon—but this time Shannon argued with more force than usual.

Devin sighed gustily. "Fine. Forgive me for caring. All I did was ask a few coworkers if they'd ever worked with him or heard of him. It wasn't really gossiping."

But her tone said she knew differently and her expression was slightly apologetic when she added, "I won't do it again."

"Thank you. Now I have to hurry or I'll be late to work."

"Yeah, guess I'll get some sleep. Uh—sorry about...well, you know."

Shannon merely nodded. Knowing Devin had meant well did not excuse the behavior. Shannon suspected James would be appalled to find out that his private life was being discussed so avidly in the hospital where he had worked so hard to establish himself in his career.

Apparently, she wasn't the only one with some dating mistakes in her past.

"Have I mentioned how nice you look tonight?" James asked Saturday evening as he held the door of the bar where his classmates were meeting for drinks and socializing. "Thanks again for coming with me."

It had been a crazy busy week for both of them with their work and her family obligations. Though they had talked a few times by telephone, this was the first time she had seen him since he'd slipped out of her bed at midnight on Monday. She'd half expected at least a little awkwardness when they'd first seen each other again, but he'd been held up at the hospital and was running a little late picking her up, so they'd started the evening in a laughing rush.

She'd hosted a fun, quirky, after-school birthday party at the ice-skating rink the day before and she chattered about that during the drive to the bar, making him chuckle a few times with her adventures on ice. He hadn't said much about his week, only that it had been busy and—his highest praise— challenging. But the discomfiture she'd dreaded had never materialized, to her relief.

She automatically smoothed a hand down the front of the full, printed-cotton skirt she wore with a deep-scoop green T-shirt. He'd assured her the occasion was casual, so she'd dressed accordingly. She enjoyed wearing skirts and colorful tops in warm weather—it made a nice change from her work uniform of khaki pants and jeans. "Thank you. And I'm looking forward to meeting your friends."

She had hesitated a few moments when he'd asked her during a phone conversation Wednesday evening to join him for this gathering. He had apologized for waiting so late to ask her. He'd explained that he hadn't planned to go himself since it wasn't really his type of thing, but he'd been persuaded by his friends.

It wasn't the short notice that had caused her pause. Nor was she particularly hesitant about mingling with a group of medical students. She was proud of both her retail work and her party business, so it wasn't that she had any feelings of inferiority in comparison. Rather, her uncertainty was due to her suspicion that James probably attracted rumors like honey drew flies.

As Devin had pointed out, he was handsome, wealthy and naturally reserved. The less he shared about himself, the more the gossips would speculate about him. She wasn't eager to be a part of that idle conjecture.

Yet, she had agreed, partially because she wanted to spend more time with James, and partially because she was curious to see him interacting with his friends. He just seemed so darn isolated in some ways, which triggered that knee-jerk sympathy for him. Was it his family background that set him apart from most people? The fact that he'd skipped so many early grades, making him younger than his classmates? His obviously genius IQ?

Or was she going to see tonight that he fit in just fine and she was simply letting her imagination run away with her?

She didn't bother to mention that he looked good, too. He always did. His gray-pinstriped white cotton shirt and gray chinos were stylishly casual, making him look as though he'd just stepped out of a men's clothing catalog. It was no wonder women's heads turned immediately in his direction the moment he walked into the crowded establishment.

His classmates had reserved a large back room for their gathering. She had asked on the way if there was any purpose for the event, but he'd merely shrugged and said the class officers wanted everyone to get together a few times during their last year of school, just for socializing. He didn't expect a large turnout, he'd added. The class was so scattered this year in various rotations and after-graduation preparations and many had family obligations by now. As he'd already mentioned, he'd considered skipping this one, but his friend Haley was one of the class officers and she'd let him know she expected to see him there.

At a glance, she could see that he'd estimated the attendance fairly well. The room was full, but not overly crowded. He'd said there were about a hundred and twenty-five people in his class, so not even a third were represented here tonight from her estimation as she mentally subtracted dates and spouses from the number of people milling around the small tables and chattering over the piped-in music.

A long table at one side of the room held assorted snacks— buffalo wings, canapés, dips and chips, a few trays of sweets that might have been brought in by the party organizers. Two servers dressed all in black with the bar's logo emblazoned across their chests worked the room, taking drink orders and stuffing what looked to be generous tips into their apron pockets.

A woman with a glossy brown bob and warm amber eyes moved toward them, followed by a sandy-haired man with an engaging grin. "James, I'm glad you could make it," the woman said.

James laughed wryly. "After you ordered me to show up or you would track me down and drag me here? I didn't dare skip out, Haley."

Haley giggled. "I wasn't quite that threatening."

"You had me shaking in my shoes." James placed a hand on Shannon's back. "Shannon Gambill, I'd like you to meet Haley and Ron Gibson, two of my closest friends."

"It's nice to meet you both."

"Nice to meet you, too," Haley replied. "We saw you at the restaurant on half-price lasagna night. We were dining with James when you stopped to say hello, but he didn't bother to introduce us."

Because his ego had still been stinging that night over her comment that he made her nervous, Shannon mused with a slight shake of her head. "Yes, I remember seeing you."

"We were at the Hayes party, too, but we stayed inside while you wrangled the kids outside. Your party was a great success. Alexis had a wonderful time."

"I'm glad," Shannon said, pleased.

"Actually, Haley and I both thought you looked familiar that night at the restaurant," Ron piped in. "We haven't met before, have we?"

"Not that I recall." She didn't add that she'd had the same feeling about James when she'd first met him at the lake, a sense that they had talked at some time in the past. Just coincidence, she was sure.

"There's my daughter's heroine." Connor Hayes approached with a mug of beer in one hand and a plate of buffalo wings in the other. "Nice to see you again, Shannon."

She smiled at him. "You, too. How is Alexis?"

"She's fine, thanks. Still carries her tote bag from the party everywhere she goes."

"I'm glad she likes it. She's such a sweet girl."

"Thanks. Mia, Anne and Liam are holding a table for us. Y'all grab some food and a drink and come sit down."

Haley sighed gustily. "The point of tonight is to mingle, not just to sit and talk with each other."

"We'll mingle after we have a drink and some snacks," James promised, nudging Shannon toward the food table.

But Shannon noted during the next half hour that the close-knit study group was in no hurry to work the room. The five of them were obviously on friendly terms with their classmates, exchanging greetings and handshakes and pleasantries when they trekked to the food tables or when anyone stopped by to speak to them, but they seemed content for the most part to spend the evening with each other.

She supposed some people might consider them a clique, but to her they were more like a little family. They finished each other's sentences, laughed at unspoken inside jokes, sympathized over each other's problems, celebrated their accomplishments, and communicated with glances and half smiles. She didn't feel left out—they were very careful to make her feel a part of the group—but she was very aware of the close bonds between this group.

Connor's wife, Mia, and Anne's husband, Liam, were accepted among them with warmth and affection, but, clearly, there was a special connection between the five who had survived the first three years of medical school together. As guarded as James was with his deepest emotions, she had no trouble seeing that he cherished these friendships.

She sensed again that he had never been part of such a tight group before, probably because he had been so much younger than classmates from his previous schools. The study group were all close in age, with no more than four or five years separating the youngest, Anne, from the oldest, Connor—gaps that made less difference in adulthood than in adolescence and college-age.

Shannon liked all of them and could see why James had grown so attached to them. She had to admit that she had been secretly a little impressed to meet Anne's husband.

"Liam McCright?" she repeated after being introduced. Eying his trademark curls and familiar, roguishly infectious smile, she'd blurted, "I've watched you on TV!"

He had responded easily to her gauche remark, setting her immediately at ease, but she still found it hard to believe at times that she was seated next to a man whose cable TV adventure travel show had made him increasingly famous. She didn't follow celebrity gossip very closely, so she hadn't realized he was married to James's friend, Anne Easton.

"How long have you been married?" she asked as they'd gotten acquainted.

Anne and Liam had exchanged an amused look, a private joke Shannon didn't understand but that the others apparently did, judging from their smiles. "Just over three years," Liam answered. "But we didn't announce it publicly until last year."

She hadn't asked any more questions about their private lives and the conversation had soon turned to plans for the upcoming months until graduation. Four of the five study-group members—James, Haley, Ron and Connor—would be out of the state for away rotations in October, and James and Anne would be away in November. Residency interviews would begin in December and continue for the next couple of months and then matches would be announced in March. Graduation would be held early in May.

"I'll just barely make it back for the Halloween party," Haley commented. "Someone else is going to have to do the prep work for that one."

"I won't make it to that one," James said, holding up his hands in Haley's direction. "You can't blame me for missing a party when I'm not even in the state."

She smiled. "Okay, you're excused from that one."

"Thank you."

"You'll be spending your thirtieth birthday all alone in Seattle," Anne said as if it had just occurred to her. "We should all try to get online that night and have a virtual party or something."

James gave her a little smile. "That would be nice."

"It sounds as though you're all going to be very busy for the next few months," Shannon commented, not wanting to think about James being gone for so long. She was getting a little too used to having him around, she thought.

The married couples shared long-suffering glances. "We're all used to that," Anne said.

Connor shrugged. "It's just the life we've chosen. Liam's schedule is packed full with his travel and writing and filming. Mia's busy with teaching and working toward her doctorate in education. I know you must have a full calendar with your party business. None of us subscribe to the theory that doctors should be placed on pedestals or given special treatment just because the career we chose is somewhat demanding."

"Hey, speak for yourself," Ron cut in with a grin. "I might like to be on a pedestal."

Haley rolled her eyes. "You'd only fall off and break your neck."

"Hey!" her husband protested while the others laughed. "I resent that."

"Get over it," Haley advised him.

He heaved a sigh and pushed his chair back from the table. "I think I'll have a couple of those cheesecake thingies. Anyone want anything from the food table?"

"I'll go with you," James offered, standing. "I wouldn't mind something sweet. Can I bring you anything, Shannon?"

She smiled up at him. "I'd take a couple of those cheesecake thingies."

"You got it. Anyone else?"

Connor and Liam decided they might as well go, too, taking orders for desserts from their wives.

Shannon watched as James moved away from her, conversing with his friends and disappearing into the crowd around the food table. He was only half a room away from her and she missed him already. That was no way for her to prepare herself for the next two months—or more—without him in her life, she thought with a hard swallow.

After all her big talk to Devin about knowing what she was doing with James, she hoped she wasn't destined to have her heart bruised by him, no matter how hard she tried to prevent it.

Chapter Nine

"I could get used to being waited on like this," Mia said with a laugh when only the women were left at the table. "Of course you know it could be a while before the men come back. Look at that group of guys gabbing by the goodies table. And they say we're the talkative ones."

"Uh-oh, looks like Margo has cornered Liam," Haley said to Anne, glancing meaningfully across the room. "Think we should go rescue him?"

Anne shook her head. "Liam is used to people wanting to be his buddy because they're impressed by his celebrity. He can handle it."

Mia focused on Shannon. "I'm glad you could join us tonight, Shannon. I've wanted to tell you again how much Alexis enjoyed her party. She's looking forward to McKenzie's karaoke party next month. I know you'll do a great job with it."

"I've been working on a pop-star theme for that one. Like the TV show? They'll be able to sing and everyone will get themed prizes like tiaras and glittery microphones and feather boas and splashy costume jewelry. The crafts project will be rhinestones and faux gems glued to picture frames. Don't tell Alexis, because it's going to be a surprise, but I'll take a picture of the group dolled up like rock stars. I'll bring a portable photo printer to make copies for all the guests to display in the frames they decorate."

"That sounds like so much fun! I would have loved a party like that at their age," Haley enthused. "My friends and I were always singing into hairbrushes at our sleepovers."

Shannon laughed softly. "My sister and I did that a few times, too."

"You're good for James," Haley commented, looking across the room to where James was chatting with the men hovering close to the sweets. "He seems to relax a little more with you than with other women he's dated in the past couple of years."

Shannon had already gotten the impression that Haley tended to speak frankly—a trait she certainly identified with. So she wasn't particularly taken aback by the comment, but she smiled and spoke lightly. "He's a nice guy. We've had fun."

"He's not an easy man to read, but we love him," Anne said quietly, her blue eyes softening.

"Not easy, perhaps, but I know he loves you all, too," Shannon replied. "He'll miss everyone next year when you're all in different places. He's told me so."

"Has he?" Haley eyed her speculatively. "Does he talk a lot to you?"

"We talk," Shannon answered with a slight shrug, not sure what Haley meant by 'a lot.'

"We really should try to get together for dinner or something next week before we leave for our rotations," Anne fretted. "To celebrate James's birthday a little early. I don't like to think about him being alone in Seattle for the occasion."

"Maybe he won't be alone," Shannon suggested. "He'll probably make some friends there."

Women friends, perhaps, she thought a little glumly. After all, there was no reason why James shouldn't go out with any interesting women he met while he was away.

Because that thought was a little depressing, she quickly spoke again. "Did any of you know that James has never had a birthday party? Not even when he was a kid? He said he's gone out to dinner with his parents and his friends, but was never thrown a real party. I guess because it's what I do that seems sad to me."

"Oh, to me, too," Anne said with a little frown.

Mia nodded. "I've never really thought about it, but we've never attended a party for James, even though he's come to many of the ones we've hosted for various events. We've had dinner with him on his birthday the last couple of years, but I guess we didn't think about a party. He never seemed to expect one—or even to want one—but maybe he would have liked it. It's hard to tell with James."

"I always assumed he'd had parties as a kid, like the rest of us," Mia commented, leaning her elbows on the table as she focused on the conversation. "I knew he was an only child, but so was Connor and his parents hosted birthday parties for him."

Haley scowled. "I get the impression his parents are sort of…well, jerky," she finished with an almost-defiant bluntness. "They don't seem to be involved in his life at all. He always seems so alone. He rarely talks about them and when he does, it's never anything critical or derogatory, but I get the impression his childhood wasn't exactly fun-filled."

Shannon thought of James's passing comment that his maternal grandmother had brought fun into his life when no one else had. She glanced quickly across the room, saw him being drawn into a conversation with someone new and took advantage of his absence to make a suggestion. "I could put together a surprise party by next weekend. It wouldn't be the first party I organized with only a few days' notice."

Haley's face lit up. Mia looked intrigued. Anne's eyes widened.

"A surprise party?" Anne asked. "For James?"

"It's just a thought," Shannon murmured, suddenly uncertain. "I mean, I could do it on short notice, but that doesn't mean the rest of you…"

"I love that idea!" Haley practically bounced in her seat. "We don't leave for our away rotations for almost two weeks. We could do it next Saturday night. We'll all be finished with this block then. Is a week enough time, Shannon?"

"It is if you can help me with a guest list. It won't be anything elaborate, of course, but we could invite anyone you think might want to come. And maybe I could send an invitation to his parents. If they're both faculty at the university, their e-mail addresses should be available at the university Web site."

"That's about the sweetest thing I've ever heard." Anne blinked rapidly, as if fighting back tears. "I wish we had thought of it, but we'll certainly help you as much as we can."

"Can we get together tomorrow and talk about it?" Haley asked with a dramatically stealthy look toward James. "We can meet at my place."

"I can meet tomorrow," Shannon agreed. "What time?"

Five minutes later, their plans were set.

"Here comes James," Haley hissed. "Everyone look natural."

Glancing from one suspiciously innocent face to the other around the table, Shannon had to stifle a grin. If they managed to keep this a secret for six days, it would be a miracle. But she was rather pleased with herself for coming up with the idea that had been so well received by James's friends.

Even if she and James never connected again after he left for Seattle, he would always remember that she had organized his first birthday party.

Leaning on one elbow, James propped his face in his hand and smiled down at Shannon. "You and the other girls seemed to hit it off tonight."

She shifted her weight against her pillow, trailing a hand down his bare arm as he leaned over her. Both of them had just recovered enough breath to hold a conversation. Her limbs felt deliciously heavy and her mind was still a little clouded from passion, but she managed to answer coherently, "I liked your friends very much."

"They liked you, too. I could tell."

"I had a very nice time tonight." She giggled softly. "Oh, and the party was fun, too."

Chuckling, he kissed the end of her nose. "What were you all talking about while the other guys and I were fetching snacks? I've never seen such guilty expressions on Anne's and Mia's faces. And Haley looked suspiciously angelic."

She walked her fingers up his smooth, nicely sculpted chest. "We might have talked a little about you. How cute you are. What pretty eyes you have. What a very nice backside you have. Has anyone ever told you you have a very sexy walk?"

He grinned. With his dark hair ruffled around his face, and a bit of a flush still lingering on his cheeks from their earlier activities, he looked more relaxed and happier than she'd ever seen him. It warmed her heart that she'd been the one to put this look on his face. She thought she'd distracted him neatly enough from his questions.

But he wasn't quite so easily diverted, even with blatant flattery. "You talked about me, huh? What did they really say?"

"They all love you," she answered candidly. "They're going to miss you when you all go your separate ways next year."

"I'll miss them, too."

"I know."

He reached up to wind a strand of her tousled red hair around one finger. "Have you ever been to Seattle?"

"No, have you?"

"No, my rotation next month will be my first visit there."

"I've heard it's beautiful. I hope you get a chance to see some of the area while you're there."

"I'd like that. Um—"

She tilted her head against the pillow, studying his face. "What?"

He met her eyes in the shadows created by the dimmed light on her nightstand. "Would there be any chance you could fly out to join me there for a few days next month?"

She moistened her suddenly dry lips. "That's very nice of you, James, but I can't."

"If it's a matter of airfare…"

"No, it isn't that," she assured him, though airline tickets to Washington were hardly in her October budget. "I've got a full calendar next month. I don't have any vacation time left from the toy store and I've got several parties scheduled, including two Halloween parties. I can't just take off on a Seattle vacation, no matter how much I'd like to do so."

"I understand."

His expression was shuttered again, so that she couldn't tell exactly how he felt about her response. Disappointed? Irritated? Resigned? Indifferent?

It bothered her that he could still hide his thoughts from

her so quickly and so easily. Every time she thought they were getting closer, he pulled away.

He'd asked her to join him in Seattle, which meant that he didn't want to say goodbye to her in a week and a half, either, right? Or was he simply affected for the moment by the pleasant evening they'd shared, followed by spectacular lovemaking? Maybe later he'd be relieved she'd turned him down. Maybe he already was—who could tell with him?

He glanced past her, toward the clock on the far nightstand. "It's getting late. Guess I'd better go."

"Do you have to work tomorrow?"

"No. It's just…well, your roommate—"

"Won't be home for several hours yet," she assured him, reaching up to wrap a hand around the back of his neck. Perhaps James was an expert at hiding his feelings, but she had never tried that hard to conceal her own. And what she was feeling now was a reluctance to waste any more of the little time she had left with James before their obligations—and probably their differences—drove them apart.

He hesitated only a moment, but then he lowered his head and covered her mouth with his. He made no effort to hide his response to the embrace. At least that was something.

James supposed turnabout was fair play. He had talked Shannon into attending a medical-school gathering with him Saturday night and she persuaded him to attend game night at her parents' house Sunday evening. He had to admit she didn't have to twist his arm. Her family fascinated him.

Stu and Karen and their three kids—Ginny, Caitlin and Jack—were there, though Stacy stayed home with her brood, including her recuperating son. There was food, laughter and general pandemonium as the adults played cards and board games while simultaneously supervising the energetic children, who were stationed on the carpeted den floor with games of their own.

As seemed to be the custom in the Gambill household, several conversations went on at one time, all at fairly high volume. Rules of the games were a bit fluid, arguments were heated but good-natured and generally a good time was had by all. James certainly enjoyed the evening.

He was even getting used to Virginia's blatant matchmaking, finding her efforts more amusing than disconcerting now. She did everything but place her daughter's hand in his, but because Shannon deflected the arch hints with indulgent humor, he was able to do the same.

"Sorry about Mom," Shannon said late in the evening when she and James went into the kitchen to make a fresh pot of decaf. "She's nuts, of course, but we love her, anyway."

"I like your mother very much."

Shannon dimpled, obviously approving his answer, despite her apologies. "She has a good heart. But she's a compulsive matchmaker, especially where I'm concerned. Don't know about you, but I've been hearing 'Kiss the Girl' playing in my mind all evening," she added with a laugh.

He didn't catch the reference. "'Kiss the Girl?'"

"You know, the song the sea creatures sing in *The Little Mermaid*, when they're trying to encourage the prince to kiss Ariel."

He chuckled. "Never saw it, but I get the gist now."

In a very pretty voice, she sang the chorus of the ditty, which seemed to be taunting a shy boy to kiss a girl or lose her.

Smiling, James reached out to tug her closer. "Well, since you put it that way…"

He lowered his head to steal a quick taste of her smiling lips.

"Oh." From the kitchen doorway, Virginia smiled smugly when James and Shannon broke apart.

"I just came to see if you need helping finding anything in here," she explained. "But I see you have everything under control."

She left the echo of her giggle behind her when she turned and hurried away.

Shannon and James shared a wry look, then burst out laughing.

After another quick card game, the adults took a break to stretch and focus on the kids for a few minutes. While three-year-old Caitlin sang a preschool song for her adoring grandparents, Shannon engaged in some horseplay with Jack, pretending to engage in a ferocious lightsaber battle. He chased her out of the room and into the hallway. A few moments later, they rushed back in with Shannon doing the chasing this time while the giggling four-year-old evaded her.

"You come back here, Jedi Jack," she threatened teasingly. "Vengeance will be mine!"

Something clicked in James's mind. He very clearly pictured a pretty, intriguing redhead chasing a little boy named Jack across a crowded fairway. The image of that redhead's brilliant smile had stayed in his mind for hours afterward, even though he'd been accompanied by another woman that evening. Elissa Copeland. Attractive, pleasant and just slightly avaricious, she hadn't fit in at all well with his group of friends. That had been his last date with her.

"Did you take Jack to the fair last fall?" he blurted to Shannon as though he expected her to follow his line of thinking.

She blinked in response to the non sequitur, but nodded. "Yes. Why— Oh, my gosh! I remember you now."

He grinned. "Jack got away from you and—"

"He ran across the fairway and you—"

"Caught him before he got lost in the crowd."

It occurred to him only then that they'd fallen into the Gambill habit of talking over each other. "I kept thinking you looked familiar that day at the lake," he said when she finished speaking.

She nodded. "So did I, but I didn't figure out why until just now."

The others looked from one of them to the other, trying to follow the garbled exchange.

"Are you saying you met before the picnic at the lake?" Virginia clarified.

Shannon shrugged. "Not exactly a meeting. We exchanged a few words at the fair last fall when James caught Jack after he got away from me."

Tilting her head in James's direction, she asked, "Were Ron and Haley there with you? They thought I looked familiar, too."

He nodded. "They were."

"And there was another woman," she recalled.

He shrugged. "Was there?" he murmured with a smile he knew didn't fool her in the least. "If so, I've completely forgotten."

"Uh-huh." She seemed to be amused by the obvious prevarication.

Finally figuring out the sequence of events, Virginia clasped her hands together. "You mean you met last year when James rescued another of my grandchildren?"

He cleared his throat. "I didn't really rescue—"

"It was obviously karma," Virginia continued, ignoring his attempt to correct her. "The two of you were fated to connect."

"Okay, let's not get carried away here, Mom." Shannon looked just a little uncomfortable now despite her indulgent tone. "We just happened to cross paths a couple of times. Just a coincidence."

Virginia waved a hand dismissively, refusing to be dissuaded from her fanciful speculation. "You were meant to know each other. That's so romantic."

"You know, it's getting a little late," Shannon said with a quick look at her watch. "I'll help you clear away the dishes and games, Mom, and then James and I have to go. We both have to work tomorrow and his day starts early."

"We have to be going, too," Karen agreed. "Got to get the kids into bed."

"When do you leave for Seattle, James?" Virginia asked while the others tidied up.

"A week from Friday. I start my rotation the first Monday of October."

"I've heard Seattle is a beautiful city."

"Yes, ma'am, so I've heard."

"Shannon's never been there, you know."

"Yes, she told me."

"Maybe while you're there—"

"I can't go to Seattle next month, Mom," Shannon interrupted, overhearing. "I have to work."

"Your boss at the toy store would probably let you take off a couple of days."

"Even if he would, I have my party business to run. I have several parties scheduled for October."

Virginia waved a hand again. "Devin could probably handle those for you. All she'd have to do is supervise the kids, right?"

For the first time, James saw a spark of temper in Shannon's eyes when she looked at her mother. "Kid Capers isn't Devin's business, Mom. It's mine. And there's a little more to it than babysitting."

"Shannon," Hollis murmured in warning while Virginia pouted. "Your mother didn't mean to insult you."

Shannon rounded toward her dad. "She wouldn't have suggested that Stu just drop everything at work to take off on an impulsive vacation."

"Hey, leave me out of this," her brother protested.

Virginia seemed about to offer an argument, but thought better of it, to James's relief. If Virginia had suggested that Stu's job as a high-school principal was more important or more demanding than Shannon's business, he thought Shannon's irritation would probably have heated into genuine anger. He wouldn't even have blamed her. He was just now beginning to understand why she complained about her family treating her like the indulged little sister who just played at life and work, no matter how hard she worked to establish her own identity.

Had he done the same when he'd suggested she take off to join him in Seattle? He shifted his feet uncomfortably, telling himself he really hadn't intended it that way. He'd simply wanted to have her with him, knowing he would miss her while he was gone. That in itself was enough of a novelty to make him reevaluate his feelings about Shannon.

The brief argument was over almost as quickly as it began. Virginia dropped no further hints and Shannon kissed her mother good-night some twenty minutes later with her usual affection. "Good night, Mom. I love you."

"I love you, too, sweetie. I'll talk to you tomorrow."

Shannon went through the same ritual with her dad, exchanging good-nights and I-love-yous—saying a variation of the words to her brother and sister-in-law, nieces and nephew, all of whom assured her they loved her, too. James shook hands with the men, swapped cheek kisses with the women and accepted surprise good-night hugs from the kids, who seemed to think he was to be included when they made the rounds before leaving.

As he climbed into his car with Shannon afterward, he tried to remember the last time he'd told his own parents he loved them, or had them tell him in return. It had been a while. They had never made a habit of saying the words, as the Gambill family did so easily. He knew his parents loved him, and that they were proud of him, in their way, though such sentiments were rarely exchanged in their household.

In the passenger seat beside him, Shannon snapped her seat belt then released a long sigh.

Fastening his own belt, James started the car. "You sound tired."

"A little," she admitted. "It's been a long day. I got up early for church service, had lunch afterward with an old friend, then had a meeting with…with a party client, and then barely had time to get home and change before you picked me up to come here. Kind of hectic."

He noticed the slight stammer, but paid little attention. She was probably still stinging a little about her mother's thoughtless dismissal of her party-business responsibilities. "I hope you know I'm aware of how hard you're working to establish your business. When I asked you to join me for a few days in Seattle, it was because I hoped you'd be able to slip away for a short time, not because I don't think your obligations here are important."

"Thanks, James. I appreciated the invitation, really. It was sweet of you to ask me to join you there and to offer to pay the airfare. Just too short notice this time."

"I understand." He didn't like it, but he understood, he added silently, ruefully acknowledging his own growing selfishness where Shannon was concerned.

Speaking of which…

"The old friend you had lunch with," he said, trying to keep his tone casual, as if he were simply continuing the conversation. "Anyone you've mentioned before?"

"No, she was my best friend in high school. She's in town on a quick trip to visit family. First chance we've had to get together in a couple of years."

She. Unaccountably relieved by the pronoun, James relaxed a little in his seat, though the extent of that relief only made him worry a little more about how hard it was going to be to say goodbye to Shannon at the end of the month.

As many parties as she had organized in the past year, Shannon couldn't remember ever being quite as nervous as she was about the surprise party for James. She and Haley, the unofficial representative from James's circle of friends, had spent quite a bit of time on the telephone making hasty decisions during the week that had passed since she'd come up with the idea. Several times during that week, she had asked herself if the suggestion had come to her in a moment of insanity. Sure, she'd performed on short notice before, but this? This was crazy!

Haley, it turned out, was a genius at organization on her end of the planning. Haley was the one who contacted James's friends with invitations, collected donations toward the party expenses and helped Shannon make final choices on options James might particularly like.

Fortunately, Shannon was a good friend to a caterer, Leslie O'Neill, whose services she used whenever possible for her parties, a favor her friend happily reciprocated for this party. Leslie decorated a cake and provided the food for the party, which was being held at Anne Easton's parents' elegant home in one of the wealthier Little Rock neighborhoods.

Anne had volunteered her parents' home and they had generously agreed. Haley had explained to Shannon that the Eastons—a prominent local surgeon and a retired family court judge—often entertained on their lawn, and had hosted Anne's friends on several occasions. James wouldn't think it at all strange to be invited there for a late-summer picnic, Haley had assured Shannon in satisfaction.

Shannon spent much of that afternoon at the Easton home setting up for the party, with the assistance of Anne and Haley. Anne's mother, Deloris, a petite blonde with a sweet smile and a slight limp left over from a stroke several years earlier—or so Haley had told Shannon—observed the preparations with interest, making an occasional suggestion based on her years of experience hosting such events.

Shannon was touched that everyone seemed so eager to make this gesture for James. It was increasingly obvious that he meant a great deal to these people, and that they respected him enormously. They acknowledged his innate reserve, but they were also aware of his kindness, his quiet competence, his generosity and his compassion. Perhaps he had a hard time expressing those qualities, but Haley confided to Shannon that his actions during their past three years of friendship had spoken for themselves.

"Our little group was sort of like a family," she expounded as she wound a streamer of silver metallic stars around one pole of the big, open-sided white tent that had been erected on the lawn. "We each had a role to play. Anne was the nurturer, who always offered a sympathetic ear when we needed to talk. Ron made us laugh when we got too stressed. Connor was the coach and the teacher—because that was his job before he started medical school. He could always explain things clearly when we didn't understand."

"What was your role?" Shannon asked, amused by the descriptions.

Haley laughed wryly. "They called me the cheerleader. I was the one who seemed to give all the pep talks when morale started dropping. The one who assured everyone there was nothing we couldn't do if we gave it our all."

"And James?"

"James was our rock," Anne said from nearby. "Calm and steady, quietly getting things done. His condo was always available for studying and his housekeeper always left healthy snacks and decadent treats to fuel us through those long sessions. The material seemed to come easily to him, but he worked right alongside us every minute, making sure we were all fed and hydrated and comfortable—he even made sure we took breaks during the sessions to play and stretch."

She could see him fulfilling that role. Taking care of the others while asking for little for himself, taking interest in their lives while sharing little of his own. Not because he was being particularly secretive, she had concluded, but because he didn't think his own life was all that interesting to the others.

The mention of his condo and his housekeeper reminded her again of the differences between their financial standings—but looking around the Easton estate, she supposed Anne could identify a bit more with James's privileged background. Money or social status had not drawn the study group together, nor had they played any part in the bonds that would probably remain between them for a lifetime, no matter how far apart their career paths took them.

Somewhat wistful now, she concentrated on finishing the preparations for the party that would show James just how much his friends—including Shannon—cared about him.

James parked in the circular driveway in front of Dr. Henry Easton's estate without a great deal of enthusiasm. To be honest, he wasn't in the mood for socializing on this last Saturday evening in September. There had been a lot of social events during the past month and he wouldn't have minded just crashing at home with a pizza and a good book that evening. Or better yet, spending a cozy, intimate evening with Shannon. He was too keenly aware of how little time remained for him to spend with Shannon before he had to leave for his away rotation.

But Anne's parents had decided to throw an impromptu send-off party for all of her friends who were leaving town for the next month and as frivolous an excuse as that seemed to be for a party, he hadn't been able to say no when Anne had practically begged him to attend. She had reminded him unnecessarily that there wouldn't be many more chances for them to all be together. She'd made it sound as though graduation was only days, rather than months, away—but she'd had a point that everything would be different for them after those degrees were awarded. So, he had accepted, hiding his reluctance with the skill of experience.

He might not have minded so badly if Shannon were at least attending this party with him. Anne had encouraged him to ask her. "We all liked Shannon," she'd added. "Feel free to bring her, if you want to."

Of course he had wanted to. It unnerved him considerably to think about how much he wanted Shannon with him—at this party and just about any other time. But she had declined his invitation, explaining that she had a party that evening. If she'd been particularly disappointed, he couldn't tell, he thought glumly.

It wasn't that he resented Shannon's work exactly. After all, his own was certainly demanding enough. While it was true he had more free time during his fourth year than he'd had before, or would have afterward, he still understood all too well how difficult it was for two people to balance their work obligations. Hadn't he seen it firsthand among his classmates, so many of whom had not been able to reconcile their hectic schedules with those of former partners?

It wasn't even as if he and Shannon had made that sort of commitment to each other, he reminded himself as he climbed out of his car and locked the door before stashing his keys in the pocket of his navy pants. She'd made it clear enough that she wasn't interested in tying herself down or sacrificing any of the independence she'd carved out for herself during the past year. She saw them as simply having fun together before James had to leave for the next couple of months—those were her words exactly, for that matter.

He'd barely seen her during the past week, though they'd spoken by phone and managed to have dinner together Wednesday night. He could almost feel the minutes he could spend with her ticking away.

At least he would be seeing her tomorrow, he cheered himself as he walked toward the side gate he'd been instructed to take to the Easton's back lawn. His parents were going to be in Little Rock tomorrow for an academic meeting at the university there and he'd talked Shannon into joining him for lunch with them. She hadn't been overly enthusiastic about it—and he could hardly blame her—but he had wanted her to meet them, maybe as a way of understanding him better. Perhaps she had accepted for the same reason.

Though the week that had just passed had been rainy, it was a beautiful evening for an outdoor party. The days were getting shorter now that fall had officially arrived. Long shadows stretched across the front lawn of the stately home as the setting sun painted the sky orange and pink. It was still warm enough that he didn't need a jacket, but he was glad he'd donned a long-sleeve cotton shirt with his chinos. There was just a hint of coolness in the air as the sun made its descent.

It occurred to him suddenly that he was the only person on the walkway toward the side gate. Quite a few cars were parked in the drive, many of which he recognized as his friends', but apparently he was one of the last to show up. He checked his watch with a frown. He was practically on the dot of the time he'd been told to arrive. Usually there were a few stragglers behind him. Ron was notorious for running late, but even his battered car was parked out front.

Odd, he thought with a frown. This whole evening had a sort of strange vibe for him, actually.

He pushed open the elaborately curved wrought iron gate and rounded the side of the house to the back lawn where he'd attended a few other events in the past couple of years. The guests certainly seemed to be quiet tonight—he didn't hear talking or laughter or music or...

"Surprise!"

He almost jumped out of his loafers. The moment he'd appeared on the lawn, a group of his friends and classmates descended upon him with the synchronized shout. With a blink of shock, he noted the white tent, the sparkling decorations, the massive cake topped with burning candles, the glittering banner that spelled out Happy 30th Birthday, James. The affectionate smiles all turned in his direction as the guests awaited his reaction. And Shannon, standing beside the cake, her red hair flaming as brightly as the candles, her brilliant smile warmer than the setting red sun.

He released the breath he had caught when they'd shouted at him in a gusty exclamation. "Holy kamoley."

Chapter Ten

"You really were surprised, weren't you?"

"I really was surprised."

"And you had a good time?"

"I had a great time. The best time of my life, perhaps."

Shannon smiled contentedly. James had assured her several times that he'd loved the surprise birthday party his friends had thrown for him, but she still liked hearing it.

She would remember all her life the look on his face when he had realized the party was on his behalf. That the shiny decorations and the beautiful cake and the balloons and gifts had all been provided for him. That his friends and classmates cared enough about him to go to that much trouble to make sure his thirtieth birthday was celebrated in proper fashion.

They had just walked into his place—the first time she'd actually seen the roomy, upscale condo. In the daylight, she knew he would have a lovely view of the red bluffs of the Arkansas River from the large balcony on the other side of spotless glass doors. Now, in darkness, the river looked like rippling black satin studded with the diamond reflections of city lights.

His decor was understated but elegant, undoubtedly styled by a professional. The colors were a bit muted for her taste, but the effect was peaceful rather than sterile. The big-screen TV and video-game systems prominently displayed in the otherwise rather formal residence should have been jarring— instead, they made her smile. Remembering the things Anne and Haley had told her about their study sessions, she could easily picture the friends relieving their stress with rowdy, shoot-'em-up games.

"Where do you want these things?" she asked, her hands filled with the gifts she'd helped him carry in.

"Just dump them on the table." He nodded toward the big dining table at one end of the open space that flowed from kitchen to dining area to living room. "I still can't believe everyone did this," he added, setting the boxes he'd carried beside the ones she deposited on the table.

She smiled at him. "They wanted to."

He searched her face with narrowed eyes. "Whose idea was it originally?"

"The subject came up while you, Connor and Ron were getting food at the bar the other night. Anne, Haley, Mia and I started talking about your upcoming birthday. I mentioned that you'd never had a surprise party and it sort of evolved from there. They asked me to put it together, which wasn't that difficult since Anne's family volunteered the venue and Haley took care of inviting people. The rest was just a matter of ordering food and cake and doing the decorating."

She laughed softly. "We didn't think you'd particularly want to do craft projects or play games, so we chose mingling, eating and roasting for tonight's entertainment."

The "roasting" part had been Ron's idea when he'd heard about the plans for a surprise party. All of the study group and a few other good friends from their class, even a couple of their favorite instructors, had prepared very funny "tributes" to James, which he had accepted with good-natured grimaces. When it had been his turn to make a speech, he had done so graciously and sincerely.

Drawing a deep breath, she plucked a flat, square, still-wrapped package from the pile of open gifts. "You have one more present to open."

He had probably noticed that there had been no gift from her at the party. Not everyone had brought presents, mostly his closest friends. Shannon hadn't wanted him to open the one from her in front of the others, so she had smuggled it in among the other items she'd carried up to his condo. "I know your birthday is still technically a couple weeks off, but since we've been celebrating tonight…"

"You didn't have to do this." His hands brushed hers when he accepted the gift, his fingers lingering over the contact long enough to make her pulse trip a little.

She had to silently clear her throat before answering, "I know. I wanted to."

She still wasn't sure she'd done the right thing by buying this gift. Not just because it had taken a sizable bite out of her budget for the next month, but also because she wasn't at all sure James would like it. She had deliberated before buying it, then again while wrapping it, even while carrying it through his door, and she still wasn't certain she'd made the right choice.

Maybe he sensed her qualms—or maybe they were written all over her face. Unlike James, she had never been very good at masking her emotions. He frowned a little when he tore away the blue-and-silver-swirled wrapping paper.

Her fingers interlaced rather tightly in front of her, she

focused intently on his face when he studied the gift, trying to read something—anything—in his unrevealing features. Feeling a little light-headed, she realized she was actually holding her breath and she made herself release it. "Well?"

He raised his dark eyes to her face and though she couldn't quite read his thoughts in them, she suddenly sensed that she had made the right choice, after all. "I love it," he said. "Thank you."

"You're sure? I don't want you to be sad when you look at it."

"It doesn't make me sad," he assured her, cradling the small, framed watercolor in his skilled hands. "My memories of my grandmother are happy ones."

She had half expected the little painting to be gone when she'd returned to the art gallery earlier that week. But the little garden scene of roses and a watering can, surrounded by a somewhat rustic, five-by-seven frame, had hung exactly where James had first spotted it. "I hoped you would feel that way about it."

"I do." There was still little expression on his face, but she thought there was just a slightly husky edge to his voice now. Possibly a sign that he was touched by her gift?

It bothered her that after all they had shared during the past six weeks, he still kept his deepest emotions hidden from her. It was just as well that she wasn't hoping for long-term from him, she told herself with a hollow feeling deep inside her chest. That would be too frustrating for her in the long run. She could tell he liked the gift, and she sensed that he was affected by her gesture, but for all she could determine from his face, it meant no more to him than the books, photo frames, pens and notepads he'd received at his party.

She supposed it was unfair of her to have hoped for more from him than he'd given those people who had known him so much longer, who had shared so much more with him than a few weeks of play and a few nights of passion. It was completely unreasonable for her to think that she and James had shared something during these past six weeks that had reached a special, formerly inaccessible part of him.

They were only having fun while he prepared to leave the state in pursuit of his future career. They'd actually spelled out the terms of their friendship—no strings, no loss of independence on either part, no plans for the future. It was exactly what she'd told herself she wanted and he needed.

An old adage popped suddenly into her head. *Be careful what you wish for. You just might get it.*

"I'm glad you like it," she said lightly. "I hope you find a place to put it. Rustic country doesn't exactly fit in with your modern decor."

But then, neither did she, she thought with a twinge of self-pity she immediately rejected. She must be more tired than usual after a hectic week and a long, busy day.

"Actually…" James set the little painting on the table and reached out to snag a hand around her waist. He pulled her toward him, his lips only an inch from hers when he finished, "I think it fits in perfectly."

Wrapping her arms around his neck, she melted into his kiss. If this was the only way she could truly communicate with James in the short time they had left together, then she would take full advantage.

Shannon was not looking forward to Sunday brunch with James's parents, and she suspected she wasn't doing a very good job of hiding it from him. She gave him an anemic-feeling smile as they approached the glass door into the lobby of the upscale downtown Little Rock hotel where they would meet the elder Stillmans. "I've heard the Sunday brunch here is amazing, though I've never tried it. Have you?"

"Yeah, a couple of times. It's good," he acknowledged.

"Don't look so nervous, Shannon, it will be fine. We won't stay all that long."

She smoothed a hand somewhat nervously down the front of the green skirt she had worn with a matching cami and a fitted, three-quarter-sleeve patterned jacket. She'd dithered over what to wear for longer than was her usual custom, finally settling on a new fall outfit that she considered nice enough to be respectful yet casual enough that she didn't look overdone. Or at least, that was the effect she was going for.

She had pinned back her red curls and covered a few freckles with a light touch of makeup, but she'd finally made herself stop fussing over her appearance. She doubted that his parents were going to make up their minds about her based on what she wore.

"I'm not even sure why I'm here," she said in a low voice to James as they crossed the carpeted lobby toward the elevators. "I mean, you and I are just friends. They understand that, right?"

"Of course," he replied a little too smoothly. "And I've got to be honest with you, I asked you along mostly because you have a talent for keeping a conversation moving. My parents and I run out of things to say to each other after a few minutes and it gets rather dull. You are never dull."

Maybe he was being uncharacteristically frank—or maybe he was trying to set her at ease with a little teasing. She laughed softly. "Well, thanks a lot. If you'd told me you brought me along to provide entertainment during the meal, I'd have prepared some ice-breaker games."

"My parents never play games," he assured her with exaggerated solemnity. "They would consider that a frivolous waste of their valuable time."

"You aren't making me feel any better about this."

"Sorry. Just want you to be prepared. My family is pretty much the opposite of yours."

That was hardly a surprise, she thought, taking a deep breath as the elevator doors swished open.

Upon meeting the professors Stillman, her first thought was that James resembled his mother more than his father. Melissa Stillman was tall, her dark hair highlighted with natural gray streaks that looked good on her, her eyes the same gleaming ebony as her son's. The same features that made James so strikingly attractive were a bit too blunt for his mother's face, giving her a slightly intimidating appearance, even though she smiled politely enough when James introduced them.

Bruce Stillman was a couple of inches shorter than his wife and several inches shorter than his son, his frame compact and wiry in comparison to James's more elegant build. His thin hair was completely gray. His face was rather gauntly carved, with a somewhat prominent nose upon which he propped a pair of half-glasses he peered over when he studied Shannon. "It's very nice to meet you, Miss Gambill."

"Please call me Shannon, Dr. Stillman."

He nodded, apparently content with the more formal address for himself. Glancing at his watch, he motioned toward the two chairs he and his wife had saved for them at the white-linen-topped table. "We expected you a little earlier. We'll have to eat quickly, I'm afraid. Melissa and I have several meetings scheduled for this afternoon."

"We were right on time, Dad," James murmured, but his father pretended not to hear.

Oh, yeah, Shannon thought with a complete absence of appetite. This was going to be loads of fun.

"So," James said as they drove away from the hotel only a little more than an hour later, "I thought that went very well. My parents seemed to enjoy the meal. I had a good time."

Sitting in the passenger seat of his car, Shannon was unusually subdued, though she nodded agreeably. "Yes, it was quite nice. The food was as good as I've heard."

He had noticed she'd barely touched her meal, a marked contrast to her usual healthy appetite. He'd attributed her lack of appetite to self-consciousness with his parents. He supposed that was understandable under the circumstances, even for someone as naturally confident and ebullient as Shannon.

Still, he decided, it had been a very civil meal. His mother had expressed interest in Shannon's business venture, and his dad—who fancied himself an expert in economics as in most other fields—had even offered a few words of advice about marketing and financial outlooks for small businesses like hers.

They'd asked a few questions about the surprise party James's friends had thrown for him the night before and his mother had thanked Shannon for sending an e-mail invitation to her university account inviting them to attend. James hadn't realized until then that Shannon had gone to the trouble of tracking them down and asking them. He could easily imagine the formally courteous response she had gotten from them conveying their regrets that they had other obligations for that evening. And he was sure there *had* been other obligations. His parents kept their calendars full of meetings and lectures and academic gatherings for months in advance. They would not change their plans at the last minute for anything as relatively unimportant as a surprise party for their thirty-year-old son.

On the whole, his parents had been quite pleasant, chatting about their colleagues, their research, their plans for a summer trip to Krakow. They'd been on their best behavior with Shannon, to his relief. He'd seen them go cold and condescending in the past with a few women he'd dated and of whom they had thoroughly disapproved. Though they'd treated Shannon with their usual reserve and slight wariness of young women who'd attracted their son's interest, they must not have seen anything in her that had roused antipathy. And really, why should they? He figured even his admittedly elitist parents could see that Shannon was a good person and that he was proud to count her as a friend.

They had wished James success in his upcoming trips, making him promise to stay in touch. He knew they were still rather disappointed that he'd chosen to go into medical practice, but they made it clear they hoped he would continue to research and publish once he entered his chosen field. He assured them that was his plan. Just because he wanted to put his skills to practical application did not mean he'd lost all interest in the study of science, he'd added with a faint smile they had acknowledged with wry glances.

When his parents had glanced at their watches simultaneously, James had taken the signal that they were impatient to move on to their next appointment. He had kissed his mother's cheek and shaken hands with his father, promising to call them the following week from Seattle. They had both shaken hands with Shannon, telling her how pleased they were to have met her. There was no mention of possible future meetings.

All in all, not so bad, he summarized, quickly replaying the entire encounter in his mind. So he had no idea why Shannon was still so atypically quiet.

"Now that we have that behind us, what would you like to do for the rest of the day?" he asked, hoping to divert her.

"I thought I mentioned that I have a meeting with a potential client later this afternoon. It's a big bash, very high profile. If I get the job, it will be a huge boost for Kid Capers."

"Yes, you did mention a meeting, but I thought it was still several hours away."

"I've got a few hours, but I need to use that time to go over my presentation. I enjoyed meeting your parents," she added in a blatantly polite fib, "but I guess we'd better call it a day when you drop me off."

"I see."

She had told him about the meeting, he reminded himself. She'd even mentioned that it would be the biggest event she had ever organized if she landed the deal, a sweet-sixteen party for the twin daughters of a prominent Little Rock family. The event was still almost six months away, but she'd assured him it would take that long to put it all together. This had seemed a little excessive to him—how could it possibly take that long to plan a birthday party?—but he'd merely told her that he had complete faith in her ability to convince the client to hire her.

He hadn't realized she would send him on his way long before her meeting was scheduled to begin.

"Maybe I could help you in some way?" he suggested, stalling for more time with her. "You could make your presentation to me, if you like—you know, a practice session."

"Thank you, but I've got it under control."

"I could—"

"I've got it, James."

His fingers tightened around the steering wheel on a surge of irritation, the first time he'd actually been annoyed with Shannon. There was no need for her to snap at him just for offering to help, he thought, aggrieved. Especially since he'd be in town only a few more days before he had to leave for the month in Seattle.

"Thanks again for the offer, though," she added as though she was aware that she'd sounded a little short.

"Sure." He pulled into her driveway. "Looks like your roommate is here, so I won't come in. Maybe you could call me later and let me know how your meeting goes?"

"Of course."

"I'm sure you'll impress them. Break a leg."

She laughed a little more naturally and leaned over to exchange a quick kiss with him. "Thanks. And don't bother getting out, I'm just going to run in and get started. See you, James."

See you. There was something very vague and unsatisfying about those words, he thought, glancing into his rearview mirror as he drove away from her house.

He realized abruptly that he'd had no idea what had been going through Shannon's mind when she had sent him away.

"So?" Devin followed Shannon from the front door to Shannon's bedroom, almost vibrating with curiosity. "How was brunch with James's parents?"

Shannon groaned and tossed her purse onto her bed. "It was a nightmare. A horrible, sixty-minute ordeal that felt as though it lasted for days."

"Oh, man." Sympathy softening her face, Devin shook her head. "Were they horrible to you?"

"Oh, no. They were very polite. *Extremely* polite."

Devin winced. "Why does that not sound good the way you say it?"

"Because it wasn't good. Honestly, Dev, they had all the warmth of a couple of glaciers. They treat James as though he were an acquaintance they like, but don't know very well—and he seems to think that's perfectly normal! They exchange pleasantries and everyone waits until the other is finished speaking before replying, rather than all talking at once like my family."

She pushed a hand through her formerly tidy hair, dislodging pins and releasing a cascade of wild curls. "Occasionally, their conversation veers into politics or obscure literary references and their idea of a joke is a barbed quote from Churchill or Oscar Wilde or some other satirist I've never even heard of. Dr. Stillman—the mother—dropped some comment about her university students being her salvation and her despair, and Drs. Stillman—the father and son—chuckled as though she'd just told a hilarious joke. I tittered like I had any clue what was so funny, but I felt like an idiot."

"'They gave her the means of supporting life, but they made life hardly worth supporting.' P. G. Wodehouse," Devin murmured.

Shannon whirled on her. "How do you *know* that?"

"Sorry, I did a paper about him in school. For some reason that quote stuck with me, because it reminded me of my English teacher…but that's not important now," Devin said hastily. "Do you think they liked you?"

"Well, let's see. When I told them my business is throwing birthday parties for children, they said something along the lines of, 'How droll.' Dr. Stillman, the father, suggested I hire a financial advisor to keep me from succumbing to the bankruptcy perils that cause most small businesses to fail. When I added that I work part-time at a toy store to help pay my bills while I establish my business, they merely blinked at me as if trying to figure out what a 'toy' might be."

"Now, Shannon, don't exaggerate."

Shannon clasped her hands to her head, which had been aching a bit during brunch and was pounding in earnest now. "You should have seen the looks they gave me when they asked where I obtained my degree."

"Uh-oh."

"Right. I told them I never finished college and I might as well have said I dropped out of junior high. People like them, with all their advanced degrees, can't imagine having no more than a high-school education. I'm sure they're secretly thrilled that James is leaving town in a few days and I won't be going with him."

"They don't really sound like your kind of people, but it is possible that you're overreacting, Shannon. They probably liked you just fine, everyone does. Maybe they just have trouble conversing with people they don't know, especially someone so much younger than themselves. From what I understand, it's always awkward meeting your kid's friends, especially...well, intimate friends."

"Trust me, it was more than that. I could tell they thought I was completely wrong for their son."

"Then they're nuts," Devin said loyally. "Besides, it doesn't really matter what they think, anyway. James is the only one whose opinion of you counts."

"James?" Shannon dropped her arms and planted her fists on her hips. "You want to know what James thought?"

"Uh—"

"He thought it went very well. He thought his parents enjoyed meeting me. He had a great time."

Grimacing, Devin muttered, "Well, it is his family. I'm sure he loves them. And he probably enjoyed introducing you to them."

Maybe, Shannon thought glumly, but as far as she was concerned, that meal had only served as proof that she and James were completely mismatched.

"Let me get this straight. You're breaking up with me?"

Shannon wrapped her arms tightly around her middle and faced James in her living room Monday evening, speaking lightly in answer to his displeased question. This was hardly the way she had hoped the after-dinner conversation she'd initiated would proceed. Perhaps she had hoped—dreaded?—that he would agree their impulsive affair had run its course, that he would be somewhat relieved she was the one bringing it to an amicable end so he didn't have to.

"It's hardly a breakup, James. That would imply we had more than a casual friendship to start with. And I still consider you a friend, by the way."

"A friend you never want to see again." His face was set in hard lines, making his eyes look like glittering onyx from beneath lowered brows.

She released a sharp sigh. "I didn't say I never want to see you again."

"You said, specifically..."

"You don't have to quote my exact words back to me with that fancy photo memory of yours," she cut in somewhat peevishly. "Essentially, what I said was, I don't think we should try to keep anything going between us after you leave for Seattle. You'll be out of the state for two straight months—"

"I'll be home for one weekend in between the two months."

"You'll basically be out of the state for two straight months," she amended impatiently. "You'll be flying all over the country in December and January interviewing for residency programs. In March and April you'll be doing more rotations here, which—"

"I'm well aware of my schedule."

"—which will keep you very busy, after which you'll have graduation and then you'll be moving a few weeks after that to start your internship," she continued doggedly, speaking over him.

This was more the style of conversation she was used to than the stuffy back-and-forth comments his family exchanged, she thought fleetingly. And though James might be more accustomed to his family's patterns, he was keeping up pretty well with hers.

"And all of that has what exactly to do with why you don't want to see me again?" he asked, his cool tone the only real sign of his agitation apart from the frown that creased his eyebrows.

"Would you stop saying that? I'm sure we'll see each other again someday. I would always enjoy hearing from you. Maybe we'll get together for dinner sometime before you graduate and you can tell me all about the great residency I'm sure you'll get into. Maybe I'll come to your graduation—I would enjoy that."

"Well, isn't that friendly and congenial."

She felt her eyes widen a bit in response to what she would almost call a savage edge to his voice now. It sounded so unlike James. "I'm just—"

He looked at his watch. "I'd better go. I have some packing to do."

He wouldn't leave for another three days, so she doubted that it would take him all that long to pack. "James, I hope you aren't leaving angry."

"Haven't you heard?" he asked flatly, turning toward the door. "Just ask anyone who knows me. I don't get angry. Or hurt or lonely or insulted or just plain old pissed off. We Stillmans believe such unseemly emotions are beneath us."

"James, wait—"

He opened the door and his expression was as completely shuttered as she'd ever seen it when he glanced back at her over his shoulder. "See you, Shannon."

She released a sad sigh when the door closed with a restrained snap behind him. That exchange had not been pleasant. In fact, it had hurt like hell.

Despite his denials, he had obviously been annoyed with her. She hadn't handled the discussion as well as she'd hoped. Or maybe he was really as take-charge and controlling as she had feared at the beginning. Perhaps he just hid it better than most people, but still wanted to be the one to call the shots, to decide when to say goodbye. In which case, her decision was even more justified.

Whatever the cause for his resentment, she noted sadly that he certainly hadn't tried very hard to change her mind.

Chapter Eleven

Seattle was as beautiful as it had been billed, lush with the greenery that had earned it the nickname The Emerald City, surrounded by water and mountain ranges. The population was as diverse as the architecture and the many parks and public attractions tempted residents and visitors alike to spend a great deal of time outdoors. A center of research and technology, the city bustled with energy and activity, yet had a generally relaxed atmosphere that set it apart from some of the other large metropolitan areas James had visited.

He could see himself living here if he decided to join the residency program at the highly respected children's hospital. He liked the facility and the staff with whom he worked during his October rotation. When he wasn't working, he explored the area, imagining himself making use of the jogging and biking trails, hiking and skiing in the towering Olympics and Cascades, sailing and kayaking on the many waterways. Yeah, he'd fit in fine here.

Of course, he could imagine himself living in Boston, too. He'd spent some time at Harvard for an undergraduate summer research program and he'd mingled as well with the slightly stuffier cliques there as he did with the Seattle crowd. He'd never had a problem getting along with people or working congenially beside them.

It was true he'd never felt as closely tied to a group as he did to his study friends in Little Rock, nor did he ever expect to feel those ties again, no matter how many friends he made in future pursuits. But he would make new friends and he'd stay in contact with the ones he already had.

I still consider you a friend.

The echo of Shannon's carefully practiced little speech whispered in the back of his head as he sat on a bench in Green Lake Park on his second Sunday in Seattle, staring blankly at a few ducks paddling in the water, oblivious to the joggers, strollers and dog-walkers milling on the paths around him. As much as he'd tried not to think about Shannon while he was more than two thousand miles away from her, thoughts of her still crept into the back of his mind whenever he let down his guard.

It was his own fault that he'd let himself get hurt, of course. She'd said from the beginning that she wasn't interested in anything long-term. Hell, she'd turned him down the first two times he'd asked her out—he should have taken the hint then.

Without undue conceit, he privately admitted that he'd never actually been dumped before. He'd been involved in a few relationships that had seemed to have promise, but had then just fizzled out—usually, he confessed uncomfortably to himself, because he had lost interest.

Reluctant to risk hurting anyone, he had confined himself for the past few years to dating women who didn't seem particularly vulnerable to heartbreak. Women like

Elissa—intelligent, competent, savvy, admittedly thick-skinned. While Shannon had been very different than Elissa, she'd had her own air of self-confidence and directness that had made him believe they could share a few weeks of fun and companionship without risk of her being hurt.

He'd been all too right about that, he thought, absently rubbing the center of his chest, where a dull pain throbbed. He'd never even imagined that he would be the one who'd walk away with both his heart and his ego in shreds.

The worst part, other than missing her so badly his teeth hurt, was that he still didn't even know what he'd done to make her send him away.

Her business was booming. If it kept up like this, she would be able to significantly cut back her hours at the toy store—or maybe quit that job altogether, Shannon thought as she studied the figures displayed on her computer screen. Kid Capers was operating in the black. Just barely, and most of the profit would be funneled back into the business initially, but modest success was within reach.

She closed the computer, satisfied with her evening's work. Standing, she stretched out some kinks and headed for the kitchen, thinking she should find something for dinner. She'd lost a few pounds in the past month and she really hadn't needed to. Her family was starting to fuss that she worked too hard. Devin was convinced she was suffering from a broken heart.

She refused to acknowledge that any of them were right.

Her life was swimming along exactly as she had planned. No one told her what to do or when to do it. Though everyone seemed to have suggestions and advice, she was the one who made her own decisions and she liked it that way.

Maybe she missed James a little—okay, maybe she missed

him a lot—but her life was still on track. She had emerged from their affair intact—mostly—and on her own terms.

But when she lay awake at night, staring at the ceiling, it wasn't her pride or independence that occupied her thoughts. Instead, she had spent too many hours wishing James had been able to share more of himself with her so she could have known how he really felt about her. She'd sensed his irritation over her clumsy attempt to put some distance between them, but had there been any more to it than that? Had she been just another Elissa to him? Someone to keep him company at parties, to warm his bed when he was in the mood, to serve as a conversation starter between him and his parents?

There were times she still thought she might have meant more to him than that—but maybe that was her own wistfulness speaking. Even if they hadn't had so many other obstacles between them—their polar-opposite families, his parents' disapproval of her educational and career choices, his career obligations, her own—that deeply ingrained reserve would have driven them apart eventually. Because of her own background, she couldn't spend her life with someone who made her always have to guess what he was thinking or feeling.

Closing the fridge without taking out any food, she wandered to the back door, looking out at the darkness of the mid-November evening. It was starting to get dark so much earlier. Winter lurked very close now, waiting to drain more heat and light from her days.

She would bet it was already cold in Boston.

"Hello, Shannon."

Kneeling on the floor of the toy store to replace a game she'd found on the floor, Shannon swiveled to look up in response to the greeting. "Haley!"

Smiling in pleasure, she stood, straightening her green

apron. "It's good to see you. How was your away rotation in...Lexington?"

"Cincinnati," Haley corrected. "Ron was in Lexington. And my rotation was great. So was his. We're going to interview in both places for residency programs."

"I hope you get the one you want. You have to be accepted, right?"

Haley nodded. "It's called matching. We list our top choices and we're matched with the programs that select us. It's a little more difficult when a husband and wife are both trying to get into programs in the same city, but it happens enough that there are protocols in place."

"And you'll learn where you've matched in March?"

"Right. Match Day. It's a big deal all across the country when every medical-school graduate learns his or her fate."

"Sounds exciting."

They were both smiling, both speaking in warm, breezy voices. Shannon suspected Haley was as aware as she was of the unspoken name hovering between them.

"Are you looking for anything in particular, Haley? Can I help you find anything?"

"I'm looking for a baby-shower gift for a friend. She's registered here for some of the infant supplies."

"Did you stop at the front and get her list?"

Haley waved a couple of sheets of printed paper in one hand. "Got it. I take it the items with an *X* beside them have already been purchased?"

"Yes. Let me take you over to that department and we'll see what's left."

"I guess you're starting to get pretty busy for the Christmas rush."

Glancing at the unusual number of customers milling in the aisles on a Tuesday afternoon, Shannon nodded. "Weekends are crazy already."

"Did you work on Black Friday last week?"

Laughing, Shannon nodded at the reference to the Friday after Thanksgiving, notorious for kicking off the holiday shopping frenzy. "We opened at 4:00 a.m. We had a line waiting for the doors to open."

"Crazy."

Shannon shrugged. "It was sort of fun. Here's the diaper bag on your friend's list."

Haley glanced at the pink-and-mint plaid bag without much interest. "Maybe I'll look at the umbrella stroller, instead."

"Sure, that's in the next aisle."

Haley studied the selection of folded strollers with a bit more interest than the diaper bags.

Drawing a deep breath, Shannon figured she might as well broach the awkward subject herself. Their avoidance was getting a little ridiculous. "Have you heard from James lately?"

"Yes, we all got together last weekend, the day after he got home from Boston. It was good to see him again after so long."

"How is he?"

Haley shrugged. "He seemed fine. He said he liked the programs in Seattle and in Boston, but I think he liked Seattle a little better. From what I could tell, anyway."

"He didn't say?"

Haley opened the stroller and locked it into position. "Not in so many words."

"Doesn't it make you crazy?"

She didn't even have to explain. Haley shot a wry smile over her shoulder as she rocked the stroller back and forth in front of her. "That James is so hard to read, you mean? It used to."

"But it doesn't now? Or have you learned how to read him during the past few years?"

"Oh, heavens, no. Not unless he wants us to."

"Then—"

"It doesn't matter. I don't have to know every thought that crosses James's mind to accept that he's one of the nicest, kindest and most decent guys I've ever met."

"Your rock."

Haley seemed pleased that Shannon had remembered their earlier conversation. "Yes, that's the way we've always thought of him."

Refolding the stroller, Haley glanced around the increasingly crowded store. "I know you're busy, so I won't keep you. But before I go…Ron and I were thinking about having a drop-in Christmas party next weekend. We'd love it if you could stop by."

"Thank you," Shannon replied gently, "but I don't think that's a very good idea."

"He misses you, Shannon."

She swallowed hard. "Has he said so?"

"Well…no."

"Has he mentioned me at all?"

"Um. No."

She hoped her smile wasn't as sad as it felt. "Then you don't really know, do you?"

"I'm pretty sure. There was just something a little off about him last weekend. Ron and I think he misses you."

"It's been two months and he hasn't even called. I think we can safely say he's moved on. And so have I."

Frowning, Haley asked, "You're dating someone else?"

"No. Between two jobs and the upcoming Christmas season, I'm too busy to date anyone right now."

Haley sighed, seeming to know when it was time to quit. "It was good to see you, Shannon."

"You, too. Tell Ron and Anne and the others I said hello, will you?"

Haley had moved a few steps away when she paused to add over her shoulder, "You were good for him, Shannon. He was as open with you as I've ever seen him with anyone."

Yet it still hadn't been enough, Shannon thought with a pang. James simply hadn't been able—or willing—to offer what it would have taken for them to stay together against all the odds.

Haley and Ron's cozy apartment was filled almost to capacity with friends and classmates drinking spiked eggnog and cinnamon-flavored hot cider and nibbling on Christmas cookies mostly purchased from local bakeries. It wasn't a formal affair, by any means, just a casual drop-in gathering to mark the end of another semester. A little over four more months and they would have their degrees, James thought, amazed by how quickly these four years had passed.

Ron and Haley stood side by side, chatting with their friend and classmate Hardik Bhatnagar. Ron's hand rested familiarly on Haley's hip as she nestled against him. On the other side of the room, Anne and Liam laughed with Connor and Mia while young Alexis admired a humorously decorated tabletop Christmas tree—Ron's contribution to the holiday decor.

Standing alone with his cup of cider, James thought about how much he had missed these people during the past couple of months. Phone calls and e-mails had not been the same as seeing them all the time—he supposed he'd better get used to that.

Over in another corner, two classmates exchanged a quick kiss under a dangling ball of plastic mistletoe. Those two had been dating for a couple of months, but James didn't expect it to last. He figured it was just a temporary fling during the relatively easy fourth year—though some people would scoff at the term "easy" being applied to any part of medical school.

He hoped they would walk away generally unscathed when the affair ended.

"You're being awfully quiet tonight, James."

He didn't realize Ron had approached him until the other man spoke. "Just taking everything in," he replied lightly. "Nice party."

"Thanks. It's the first time Haley and I have actually entertained, you know. It's not so hard if you use bakeries and delis for the snacks and buy your decorations at the local discount store."

James chuckled. "None of that matters as much as the chance to get together with friends."

"That's what we figured. So, how come you're here by yourself? You know you could have brought a guest."

James shrugged. "No one I particularly wanted to bring. I'm having a nice time on my own."

Ron cleared his throat. "So, have you called her since you've been back in town?"

It was tempting to prevaricate by asking blankly who Ron referred to. Instead, James merely shook his head and took another sip of his cider. "I'm sure she's very busy this time of year," he said after swallowing the hot beverage. "It's a hectic time for both retail and party businesses, I would imagine."

"I bet she'd like to hear from you."

"I doubt it." It took a bit more effort than usual to hide the pain and regret he still felt whenever he thought of Shannon. "Apparently, I wasn't her type."

Eying him over the rim of an eggnog mug, Ron murmured, "I wouldn't have thought Shannon was *your* type."

Staring at the plastic mistletoe, James replied with uncharacteristic candor, his tone bleak to his own ears. "You'd have been wrong."

After a moment, Ron asked somberly, "Did you ever tell her that?"

"Not in those words."

"Uh-huh. You thought she could read minds? Because, face it, my friend, she'd have to be a psychic to know what you're thinking most of the time."

James gazed down into the dregs of his cider. Oddly enough, he thought he had learned from Shannon and her charmingly open family how to communicate a bit more effectively. Comparing her family gatherings to his own, he had realized that the rather formal manners that had been drilled into him, while very useful in their place, tended to hold others at a distance in most settings.

He wasn't sure what had made the idea click in his head, but it had finally occurred to him that what Shannon referred to as his "doctor face" had been his tendency to fall back on that formality whenever he was in a professional setting. It hadn't been such a problem for him in academia, but dealing with frightened or stressed patients and their families had required a slightly different approach.

He would probably never be as easily approachable as Shannon or the other Gambills, but he'd worked on being a little less solemn in his physician role and he thought he was making progress. He'd had few criticisms of his communication skills in his evaluations from the Seattle and Boston programs. There had been one comment from a ponytailed, aging hippie attending physician in Seattle that James could stand to "loosen up" a little, but other than that, he was going to be a superb doctor.

Shannon deserved the credit for helping him in that respect, James thought now. Too bad she would probably never know what she had done for him in those few weeks they had been together.

The week-old newspaper article had been handled so much that it was already starting to shred a little around the edges.

Shannon was glad she'd stashed a few copies away for mementos and scrapbooks. She just couldn't seem to stop admiring this one.

The brief article had run in the features section of the local newspaper last Thursday. Buried inside the section, it was hardly a headline story, but she didn't care. There was a pretty decent photo of her wearing a wizard's robe and leading a mixed group of birthday-party guests in a well-received game she had created for the event and a nice write-up of some of the services she offered through Kid Capers party planning. She'd booked three more parties in the next four months as a result of the publicity. The new year was definitely starting out well from a business perspective.

Refolding the page, she set it aside on her business table and stood, stretching out kinks in her back. Now that the Christmas season was behind her, she had cut back her hours at the toy store a bit, but today had been a long one. She'd barely had time to eat lunch. She headed for the kitchen, deciding to dig out the leftovers from a veggie casserole Devin had made for them yesterday.

To her family's expressed satisfaction, she'd gotten her appetite back during the holiday season and had regained a couple of the pounds she'd lost in October and early November. She knew she looked healthier and happier. They would never know the effort it had taken for her to get to that point.

Christmas had passed in a blur of work, parties, rowdy family gatherings and preparations for the new business year. She'd been entirely too busy to spend much time brooding about…about any personal issues, she amended quickly, not wanting to set off thoughts of anyone in particular. Now, at the end of the second week of January, her schedule was slowing enough that she had to make a special effort not to dwell on how much she still missed that one person she tried not to think about.

Shouldn't the ache have eased by now? Since she was the one to have called it quits, should she really be this empty and disappointed? It hadn't been at all like this after she'd broken up with Philip. All she'd felt then was a mixture of relief and chagrin that it had taken her so long to act. She hadn't been haunted by her memories of him. Hadn't wondered where he was or who he was with. Hadn't found herself hoping he was happy and yet secretly wishing he was miserable without her.

She was doing fine, she told herself in a little pep talk that was by now very well rehearsed. She was quite content to be on her own, savoring the independence that meant so much to her. If, eventually, she met someone who could share her life without overshadowing her, that would be lovely. Someone who could appreciate her accomplishments while celebrating his own. Someone who offered advice but didn't get offended when she decided not to follow it, and who occasionally asked advice from her in return, acknowledging her own competence and intelligence. Someone who shared his feelings with her— his hopes, his dreams, his fears and sorrows—and provided a sympathetic ear for hers.

It would have been absolutely perfect, she thought wistfully, if James had proved to be that person.

She was almost finished with her reheated meal when someone rang her doorbell. Startled by the sound, she glanced at the clock displayed on the microwave. Just after 8:00 p.m. Devin wouldn't be home from work for another eleven hours and Shannon wasn't expecting anyone else to drop by tonight. It had to be someone from her family, she decided, moving toward the door. No one else she knew would just show up like this without calling first. She hoped nothing was wrong.

A dozen unnerving possibilities—several of them involving

her nephew Kyle—swirled through her head when she peeked cautiously through the curtain to see who pressed the door-bell for a second time. The one possibility she had not even considered was that she would see James Stillman standing on her front step.

The curtain dropped from her suddenly nerveless fingers. Her mouth went dry, making her wonder if she could speak coherently even if she managed to open the door. Drawing a deep, unsteady breath, she ordered herself to get a grip.

She pushed a hand quickly through her hair before turn-ing the lock, deciding there was nothing she could do about her slightly crumpled work clothes of white shirt and khakis. Pasting on a faint, politely curious smile, she opened the door. "James. This is a surprise."

His appearance hadn't changed at all in the past ten weeks and three days since she'd last seen him. Not that she'd been counting. And not that there was any reason he should look any different, she added with a mental wince at her own fool-ishness.

His dark eyes searched her face. "I should have called first."

"That would have been nice," she agreed lightly, "but as it happens, I've got a few free minutes. Come in."

"Thank you." He carried a small, plain brown shopping bag in one hand, but he made no reference to it when he stood in the middle of the living room, looking uncharacteristically ill at ease. "How have you been, Shannon?"

"Busy. You know—the holiday season. Crazy."

He nodded, apparently following the disjointed response without much effort. "I've been out of town the past week. Combined some interviews on the east coast—New York, Boston, Baltimore. Someone showed me the newspaper article about your business this afternoon. I wanted to tell you I saw it and that it was great. Should be a big boost for Kid Capers."

That was why he'd come? Because a random newspaper article had reminded him of her? "Yes, I've gotten several calls as a result of the free publicity."

"You looked very nice in the picture. The kids seemed to be having a great time."

She nodded. "I was proud of the way it all turned out."

"You should be. I know how hard you work to make those parties look effortless."

There were few compliments he could have given that would have pleased her more. "Thanks. That's exactly what I hope to accomplish."

She motioned toward the couch. "Would you like to sit down? Can I get you anything?"

Maybe he really had come by just as a friendly gesture. After all, she was the one who had expressed a desire to remain friends. She'd even suggested they could get together sometime for dinner or something, hadn't she? Of course, she hadn't expected him to actually take her up on it. Nor for him to show up unannounced at her doorstep after he'd left in such umbrage the last time she'd seen him.

He glanced at the couch, but made no move toward it. "I won't stay long. I'm sure you have things to do. I just wanted to tell you I saw the article and I'm very proud of what you've accomplished. And to give you this, if you'll accept it," he added, offering the small bag.

Mystified as to what she would find, she took the bag and dug into the tissue wrapping. Her heart clenched when she lifted out the gift.

She remembered this scarf. Remembered the way his hands had felt on her shoulders when he'd wrapped it around her, the way he had smiled when she stroked her own hands appreciatively down the colorful fabric that had been woven on a loom in Ecuador. "It's the one we saw in the River Market store."

"Yes. I bought it for you the next day because you seemed to like it, but the time never seemed quite right to offer it. I… well, this probably isn't the right time, either, but I wanted you to have it. Call it a congratulations on your business success, if you like."

"I don't know what to say."

"Just say you like it," he suggested gently. "It's too late for me to take it back now and it really doesn't match any of my clothes."

She forced a smile, deciding it would be ungracious to refuse the gift. Her fingers buried tightly in the fabric, she spoke a bit huskily, "I like it very much. Thank you, James."

She would keep the scarf as a memento of the time they had spent together, she told herself. She suspected there would always be both pleasure and pain when she looked at it.

She thought he saw a flicker of relief in his expression when he nodded. "You're welcome. I'll go now, I just wanted to…"

"Wait." She spoke quickly to stop him as he moved toward the door. "I…how did your interviews go?"

It was a lame attempt at stalling him, but she couldn't bear to let him leave just yet. She wanted just a few more minutes with him, she thought longingly. Not nearly enough, but she would take what she could get.

"Fine. I saw some very interesting programs."

"So you won't know until March where you'll end up?"

He shook his head. "I have to turn in my list, arranged by preference, in a couple of weeks. The match will be made from that list."

"Have you decided on your first choice yet?"

"I'm still making up my mind."

"I see." She struggled to see any hint of his thoughts in his shuttered eyes. Was it hard for him to leave her this time?

Was he hoping she would ask him to stay? Had he missed her at all during the past ten weeks and three days?

Growing frustrated with the futile effort, she finally decided to ask outright, "How are you, James? Is everything going well for you?"

A muscle clenched in his cheek, and her breath caught. There had definitely been...something in his expression.

Whatever it was didn't affect his voice when he replied, "I'm fine. My rotations went well. I got pretty decent evaluations, actually—even in my communications skills."

She wanted to believe she'd had at least a little to do with that, though she didn't know if James would agree. "Congratulations."

"Thanks. I did listen when you offered tips," he surprised her by adding, as if he'd heard her thoughts. "I've been working on that 'doctor face' that people seem to find too intimidating."

She took a step closer to him, her gaze locked with his. "That's great. But there's something else. Something that's bothering you."

She sensed it now in the same way she'd once guessed she'd hurt his feelings with a throwaway comment about him making her nervous. Something was causing James pain. He was trying to hide it, but she detected just a hint of a crack in his emotional veneer. "What's wrong?"

He hesitated a few moments and she thought she might have surprised him with the insight—as she had startled him when she'd read him that first time. And then he glanced down at his empty hands and admitted, "I have been sort of down this week. My cousin died a couple of days after Christmas. Pneumonia. It took her very quickly."

Her chest clenched painfully. "Oh, James. Kelly passed away? I'm so sorry—for you and for your poor aunt."

He nodded. "We'd been braced for this for a while. Kelly's

health has been very fragile for the past year. But…well, it's hard to say goodbye. Hard for a doctor to admit there was nothing more that could have been done."

"How is your aunt?"

"She's doing as well as can be expected. She's spending a few days in Fayetteville with my parents. Mom's been very supportive of her sister through this ordeal and even Dad has been surprisingly sympathetic. He and my aunt aren't exactly buddies still, but he's staying out of the way for a few days so she can spend time with Mom."

"I'm glad they have each other." But who did James have? She rested a hand on his arm and repeated, "I'm so sorry."

"Thanks, Shannon." Only the faintest of husky undertone gave a clue to his emotions. He shifted his weight toward the door again. "I guess I'd better—"

Her fingers tightened on his arm. "James. Why did you come here tonight?"

His brows twitched downward for only a moment before he replied, "I told you. I saw the newspaper article and I wanted to congratulate you. And to give you the scarf."

She shook her head and inched a bit closer to him so she could look him straight in the eyes. "Why did you come here *tonight?*" she repeated.

"I—well, I guess I just wanted to see you."

"Why?"

He moistened his lips, looking more uncertain than she had ever seen him. "I've missed you," he said simply.

"You could have called."

"I wasn't sure you'd want to hear from me."

"No, that doesn't cut it. Why did you come here to-night?"

She knew she was badgering him and that he wasn't sure what she wanted, but she couldn't seem to stop. If James walked away now, it really would be over between them. But even more importantly, she sensed that if he left now, if he buried his feelings again this time the way he always had, he would never break through the emotional barriers his parents had built around him. He had so much to give, so much potential behind those rigid walls—but if he didn't find a way around them, she was afraid he would end up alone and unhappy.

She supposed he could find someone like his parents, someone who would be content to live the way they did, engaging their intellects while suppressing their feelings, feeding their brains and starving their hearts. She couldn't bear the thought of James giving up and doing the same. He had admitted more than once that he had tried very hard not to be like his parents, despite his fondness of them.

She looked fixedly up at him, willing him to communicate with her. To truly connect with her.

And suddenly, it was as if the curtains lowered for only a moment behind the dark surfaces of his eyes, giving her a brief look at what lay behind. The glimpse of pain, of isolation and loneliness broke her heart.

"I needed you," he said simply.

He wasn't the only one who had to accept some hard facts, she realized abruptly. She had made some foolish mistakes herself. She'd been so stubborn in insisting she didn't need anyone in her life that she had been completely blind to the fact that maybe James had needed her. And that just maybe she needed to be needed.

"I'm sorry," he said with a slight shake of his head. "I shouldn't have—"

Rising onto her tiptoes, she wrapped her arms around him, clinging tightly. After only a moment, his own arms went around her and he buried his face in her hair.

"I'm so sorry you're hurting," she murmured into his ear. "I know you're sad."

He nodded into her hair, his face still hidden from her. "I just wish there had been something I could have done for her," he muttered. "My aunt called me, begged me to come. All this training, all this education—and she still slipped away with me and two other doctors standing right there beside her bed."

She blinked back a surge of hot tears, knowing this wasn't the time to shed them. "You won't be able to save them all, James. You know that intellectually. Now you have to accept it emotionally."

He nodded again.

"It hurts you so badly this time because she was your cousin and you loved her," she added quietly. "You'll be an even better doctor because now you'll understand how your patients' families feel. You'll never again see your patients as challenging puzzles or interesting medical cases. You'll see their hope and their fear and you'll remember Kelly. You'll empathize with the people who place their trust in you and they'll find reassurance in your caring. And for all of those you save, you'll understand exactly how much suffering you prevented because you chose to put your knowledge and your skills into practice."

Her vision was still blurred by a film of liquid when she drew back a little to look at him. His eyes were dry, but still seething with his grief and frustration. "You'll be such a wonderful doctor, James."

He drew a long, deep breath, his eyes slowly clearing. But maybe they weren't quite as shuttered as they usually were? Maybe he was letting her see just a little more of his thoughts, whether intentionally or because he was too weary to hide them completely?

"I didn't mean to burden you with this tonight," he muttered, pushing a hand through his hair.

"I'm sure your parents are brilliant people, James, but they're full of beans in some ways."

One corner of his mouth twitched in a the faintest semblance of a smile in response to the apparent non sequitur. "I know."

"No matter what they've told you all your life, there is no shame in expressing your sadness about losing your cousin. Nor in turning to someone else for comfort in that grief. Maybe they've coming around to that realization by offering their home to your aunt at this time. Or maybe not, but that doesn't mean *you* have to keep pretending that nothing in life affects you on more than an intellectual level. It isn't a sign of weakness to admit that you have feelings. That you have needs."

After what might have been a brief, internal struggle, he said in a low voice, "I need you, Shannon. More than my next breath. I haven't felt really alive since you sent me away. I kept trying to convince myself that you were better off without me—and vice versa, perhaps—but I never stopped missing you and wanting to be with you."

"I was an idiot," she admitted, her heart clenching in both nerves and joy. "I panicked after that stilted brunch with your brilliant, reserved parents. I was afraid you'd start expecting me to be like them—and I knew I just couldn't."

"*I* don't even want to be like them," he said forcefully. "I love them—they're my parents, Shannon. My family. But I don't want to be them. I thought you sent me away because you'd grown bored with me. Because my family and I were too dull and uninteresting in comparison to your colorful family."

She nearly choked. "Bored? With you? I can't see that ever happening, James. It would take a lifetime just to get to know everything there is to learn about you."

"I feel the same way about you," he said, pulling her toward him again. "And I've always enjoyed the learning process," he added in an attempt at a joke.

She held him off for a moment. "I'm crazy about you," she said candidly. "I have been from the start, as terrifying and ill-fated as it seemed. But—"

"But you want to be your own person. To run your own life. To make your own decisions."

"Well, yes, but—"

"You don't want to change who you are for me or anyone else."

"Right. But—"

"You need—"

"James. Let me talk. You sound like a Gambill."

He looked rather pleased by the comparison, even though she had not meant it entirely as a compliment. "What do you want to say?"

"I was just going to say, I don't want to rush into anything," she replied somberly. "I'm crazy about you—but I want to take it slowly and make sure we do this right. I've failed at relationships before. I can't bear the thought of failing with you."

"We'll take it slowly," he promised, his lips hovering over hers. "I can already predict it's going to get complicated. Just promise me you won't give up on me again."

She locked her arms around his neck, pressing full length against him as she rose on tiptoe to close the slight gap between them. "I won't give up on *us*," she whispered against his lips.

He expressed his satisfaction with a long, thorough kiss.

For once, he was almost completely open to her. She felt the sadness in him. The uncertainty and the fears. The relief, the hopeful joy. He would lock those emotions away again soon. That was just who he was, she thought, and she didn't want to change him, really, any more than she could change to please him. But perhaps he had just given her the key to unlocking his feelings when she needed him to share.

It seemed that the key had been hidden all this time in his heart.

Epilogue

Graduation was held the second weekend in May in an arena at the local fairgrounds, one of the few places in the area big enough to seat all the graduates and their families and guests. Physicians, nurses, pharmacists, technicians, researchers and other graduates in the medical sciences sat in folding chairs on the arena floor dressed in black caps and gowns with hoods and tassels color-coded to match their individual disciplines.

Medical students wore green velvet hoods hanging down the back of their gowns. They'd received those hoods at the honors convocation the night before. Sitting in the bleachers with her family on her right and James's parents and aunt Beverly on her left, Shannon kept an eye on James as he sat in his folding chair waiting for his name to be called.

"I've lost James again," her mother, who sat at Shannon's right side, complained. "They all look just alike sitting out there in those caps and gowns. Which one is he again?"

While Stu pointed out James to their mother, Shannon turned her attention to James's mother, who sat at her left. Melissa fanned her face with a thick program. "It's warm in here. Bruce and I should have skipped this event. The hooding ceremony last night was the more important program. And it isn't as if we haven't watched James receive three other diplomas before this one."

The crowd milled and talked in the bleachers, making it hard at times to hear the names being droned from the stage. After several speakers and more than a hundred names that had already been called for various degree presentations, the audience was growing restless.

Last night's hooding ceremony for the M.D. graduates had been solemn and formal, but it turned out that medical-school graduations were as cheerfully disorganized as any high-school ceremony Shannon had ever attended. Hoots and cheers and the occasional blast of an air horn from various family groups in attendance caused James's father to scowl and mutter about "rowdy yokels."

"I think he would have been disappointed if you weren't here," Shannon confided quietly to Melissa. "He has said many times that he credits you and his father for setting such a good academic example for him to follow."

Melissa preened just a little. During the past few months, Shannon had discovered that both Melissa and Bruce were highly susceptible to flattery. If that was what it would take to have an amicable relationship with James's family, then Shannon was prepared to spend quite a bit of time in her future stroking their egos.

She applauded enthusiastically for Anne and Ron and Haley and Connor when their names were called. One by one they crossed the stage, their heads held high beneath the flat-topped caps, the pride of accomplishment in their posture. After quite a few more names were called in alphabetical order, it was finally time for James to be recognized.

"Dr. James Stillman," a sonorous voice intoned over the speakers and James stepped onto the stage.

"Wooohooo, James!" Stu yelled, pumping the air with his fist. J.P. hooted in unison. The rest of the Gambill family cheered and applauded energetically.

Their own restrained applause overshadowed by Shannon's family, James's parents looked startled. Bruce appeared about to fade into his seat in response to the amused attention the Gambills had drawn to them. Shannon smothered a smile as she wondered how he felt about his son's second family being filled with "rowdy yokels."

Was she mistaken or was Melissa a little amused by the Gambill family's vocal support of James? Shannon thought she might have seen the faintest hint of a smile curve the older woman's lips for only a moment. On the stage, James accepted his rolled diploma, shook hands with the faculty and administrators lined up along the way, then paused at the top of the steps to look in their direction and give a thumbs-up, earning another cheer from Stu and J.P.

"Undignified," Bruce grumbled, while Melissa fanned her face a bit more furiously, her lips twitching again.

Pandemonium reigned on the fairgrounds surrounding the arena when the ceremonies concluded. People rushed to cars, milled on the sidewalks, hugged, chattered and snapped pictures. Before turning in their caps and gowns, the study group gathered on a grassy rise behind the arena to pose together. The five of them stood proudly, arms interlocked, diplomas on display while their spouses and family members memorialized this milestone in numerous digital photos.

They looked happy, Shannon mused, studying the five friends with a lump in her throat while she snapped her own pictures. Excited. Eager. And just a little melancholy, as each acknowledged this was the end of an era for them.

Their friendship wasn't ending, but it would be different beginning next week. Now that Match Day was behind them, they knew exactly where they would be spending the next three-to-five years, depending on their specialties. Anne, who wanted to specialize in women's gynecological surgeries, would be moving to Baltimore with Liam, who could be based anywhere and still pursue his cable TV and writing careers. Ron and Haley had been accepted into programs in Lexington, Kentucky—Ron in pediatrics, to be followed by a hematology and oncology fellowship, Haley in a triple board program in psychiatry, child psychiatry and pediatrics. Connor was staying in Little Rock to train for family medicine.

As for James—

She smiled mistily up at him when he moved beside her and slipped an arm around her. "Hi, Dr./Dr. James Stillman," she teased him, referring to his two postgraduate degrees.

He chuckled and dropped a kiss on her nose. "Hello, Shannon Gambill-Stillman, CEO of Kid Capers, Inc.," he joked in return.

Despite her insistence in January that they not rush into anything, Shannon and James had been married for almost a week now. It had taken all her organizational skills to put together a wedding in just over a month, but she had managed. James had proposed on Match Day, after the raucous party at a local pub where all the class members' matches had been announced. Conceding that she didn't need any more time to be sure she wanted to spend the rest of her life with James, she had accepted.

They'd married in the church her parents had belonged to for many years, followed by a country-club reception attended by many family members and friends. They could have waited to be married after the graduation ceremony, but they'd decided to leave for their honeymoon the following day, giving themselves time to savor being together before James had to dive into his residency.

She thought she would enjoy living in Seattle, establishing a branch of Kid Capers there while Devin took over the business here. James would be busy with his residency and she would be equally busy with her own pursuits. They would be each other's most fervent supporters, their safe haven from the madness. She was both nervous and extremely excited about the adventures awaiting them.

It would be a while before her business would be solvent there, she admitted realistically, but like her husband, she had always enjoyed a challenge.

"I love you, James," she murmured, gazing happily up at him.

He looked down at her with that faint little smile that would always make her pulse race. "I love you, too."

It was becoming easier for him to say all the time. And she believed him implicitly. It was written all over his face.

* * * * *